On November 1st, 2008, iconic underground comix artist and bon vivant S. Clay Wilson was found unconscious between two parked cars, somehow surviving severe bleeding in three hemispheres of his brain. He spent a year in the hospital but will never fully recover. He has stopped drawing, struggles with any task that requires short-term memory and needs 24/7 care.

The S. Clay Wilson Special Needs Trust has been set up to help Wilson, an artist who gave the world so much, in his hour of need.

In tribute to the patron saint of Bay Area misfits, 10% of each copy of this book sold will be donated to the Trust.

For more details, please visit **www.SClayWilsonTrust.com**

Donations to the Trust can be sent directly to:

P.O. Box 14854
San Franscisco,
CA 94114

PRAISE FOR BOB LEVIN'S EARLIER WORKS

THE BEST RIDE TO NEW YORK

"Sensitive, sad, and … superbly written."

— ***New York Times Book Review***

"The most striking first novel since … *The Friends of Eddie Coyle.*"

— ***San Francisco Chronicle***

"Rhapsodic tones that sometimes remind of Kerouac, sometimes of Hemingway … similes nearly worthy of Raymond Chandler."

— ***New York Daily News***

FULLY ARMED

"A fascinating exploration of truth, friendship, and survival."

— ***Booklist***

"Truly intriguing … a disquieting hybrid, a mystery story combined with philosophical meditation." — ***East Bay Express***

THE PIRATES AND THE MOUSE

"Compelling … fascinating and informative. Chronicles a riveting segment of American cultural history. An important story."

— ***The Onion***

"Rollicking … The treat of Levin's book lies in the Merry Prank-sterish narration, equal parts smartass opinion and conventional reportage." — ***Salon***

OUTLAWS, REBELS, FREETHINKERS & PIRATES

"An unassailably great book … (Levin) may be the best comic critic writing today."
—*Rain Taxi*

"Bob Levin is a great writer and this is a beautiful book."
—*Journal Of The Lincoln Heights Literary Society*

MOST OUTRAGEOUS

"Lurid and fascinating … loathsome … and compelling"
— *Utne Reader*

"The most challenging and thought provoking book I read last year … It is painful to read and impossible to forget."
— *The Oregonian*

"An even, calm, and sane book about a wild, empassioned and nutty subject. … Levin is always worth reading … he found a story dark, complicated, and strange enough to get him writing consistently at the top of his range."
—*Reason*

CHEESESTEAK THE WEST PHILADELPHIA YEARS: A REMEMBOIR

"Despite the chatty, bouncy, self-deprecating style of the early stories of *Cheesesteak*, there is an artistic sensibility at play on every page … an inherent honesty … The later years of *Cheesesteak* take on a hurried gravitas, poet-touched."
— *Broad Street Review*

THE SCHIZ

a novel by Bob Levin

Spruce Hill Press
Berkeley, CA

Spruce Hill Press
P.O. Box 9492
Berzerkeley, CA, 94709

This book is a work of fiction. Names, characters, places, incidents and events are either creations of the author's imagination or are factoids used fictitiously in the pursuit of a greater truth. Any resemblance to actual persons undead, living or dead, is purely coincidental.

First paperback edition, September 2016
Edited and packaged by Milo George

ISBN: 978-0-9972214-0-4

Printed in Mattoon, IL USA
by United Graphics, LLC

www.TheBobLevin.com

For Adele,

it goes without saying,

But I also wouldn't've finished this
without Milo's encouragement and help.

INTRO

Author's Introduction.

In the late 1970s, I envisioned myself writing short stories in the sophisticated, witty, macabre manner of John Collier and Roald Dahl. That only one of these stories — concerning a homicidal mechanical pool cleaner — found a home outside my filing cabinet was somewhat discouraging. So was the fact that the periodical which welcomed it featured colored photographs of nude women with Triple-D cup breasts and abdominal surgical scars and contained ads for, not one, but three types of penis enlargers. When my mother sought to buy a copy of this periodical, the newsstand operator provided her a brown paper bag within which to carry it away. My second best story of that era had its origin in my representation of an applicant in a workers' compensation claim about whom I had a conversation with an evaluating psychiatrist similar to the one Princeton Gutkin has with Morgan Beaujack in chapter II herein. That story continued to intrigue me, even after my writing aims had turned elsewhere.

This story began to grow to novel length in 1987 when, for the first and only time in my life, I was part of a Writers' Group. And that came about because of a phone call I received from a woman I will call Harlene. Harlene was an acting instructor (a disciple of Julian Beck) and the author of a biography of Lupe "The Mexican Spitfire" Velez, who now desired to write fiction. A self-described "superb networker," she already had Rolodexed the names and numbers of two dozen East Bay residents who publicly displayed one career but, like myself, stashed away another, as a writer, in the closet. She hoped to forge a crackling group out of such split souls, and, should I wish to be included, would interview me to see if I merited membership.

My wife, herself a writer and psychotherapist, and who, in retrospect I think, was probably being driven batty by the groans and silences and mangled sheets of paper issuing from my study, thought a group would be good for me. So I met Harlene, who turned out to be in her early forties, slightly overweight, and have pixie-cut, green-tinted hair, for coffee at a now defunct Brazilian place in downtown Berkeley. (In the spirit of gentlemanly fairness, let me describe myself as several years older, eye-glassed, grey-bearded, and bald as a Cheese Board baguette.) We hit it off just fine. We both admired Flannery O'Connor and Nathanael West, and her ex-brother-in-law (who, fortunately, had taken her side in her divorce) had played in the same pick-up basketball game as I in the early '70s. I was in.

"Great," I said. "I'm looking forward to it."

"We'll meet in two weeks at my house. Will Tuesday be good?"

"Perfect."

"Any chance you could have twenty pages ready by then?"

"There is this story I'm thinking of turning into a novel. I'll try to work up a portion of that."

At our inaugural meeting I presented my group-mates with what was then the first two chapters. This is what they said:

"Sleazy."

"*Disgusting.*"

"*What* kind of book is this?"

Then, when they had loosened up ...

"I could not understand what these people had to do with one another."

"I didn't know what anyone was talking about."

"Your characters left me feeling so unclean I didn't want to spend another moment in their company."

Not one "sophisticated" in the bunch. The current opening did not then exist, but I doubt the burning caterpillars would have swayed any opinions.

I was shocked. My "credits" were superior to anyone's in the room. (Harlene had had us run them by each other by way of introduction.) I was always the best (or second best) writer in any class I took. And this was, for God's sake, *Berkeley*! These were Berkeley *writers*! These were such *very* Berkeley writers that I had quickly found myself wondering what quirkiness Harlene had tumbled to in me that made her think I would fit the mix. She, herself, was composing stories about a fortyish acting teacher who has affairs with her sixteen-year-old daughter's skate-boarding friends. Arnold, a six-foot-five, two hundred-ninety pound, skin-headed jingle-writer for an advertising agency, specialized in "prose poems" in which the conjunction of word-against-word took precedence over larger organizational units, such as sentences or paragraphs, and rang out lines like "Bi-cuspid ripping breast; lamb-juice sinking upon elevator carpet." (He was pretty good, actually.) And Daphne, a pre-school instructional aide, who dressed like she was auditioning for the role of Mountain Girl in a forthcoming Ken Kesey bio-pic, wrote "autobiographical science-fiction about mutants." I felt like a fiendishly inverted chorus inside my head had broken out into "If you can't make it here, you can't make it anywhere" and was kicking up its heels in my cerebellum.

I went home. I thought it over. I talked to Adele. And she remembered an anecdote a professor of ours at San Francisco State, Arthur Foff, once told. According to Foff, early in the writing of *Remembrances of Things Past*, Marcel Proust succumbed to the hounding of a prominent Parisian critic and gave him a portion of his manuscript to read. When they next encountered each other at a cafe, the critic said, in so many *mots*, "Not bad, Marcel, but too heavy on the description." Aha! Thought Proust. So that is what I have going for me.

Aha! I thought. And wrote my next two chapters.

Harlene kicked off the second meeting by asking if I would mind sharing my reaction to the previous week's comments.

Not at all, I said. I told her I had thought a great deal about them. (True enough.) I told her I appreciated the honesty and sincerity of the convictions expressed. (I was being generous to myself here.) And I told her about Proust. "So," I summed up proudly, "I'm not changing a word."

Harlene told me I was being close-minded and defensive.

Then we discussed Harlene's story. Arnold praised its "surreal" quality. Daphne commended its "seizing of the power." I mentioned two or three things I liked and four or six I didn't.

Harlene told me I was being hostile, negative and couldn't appreciate the complexity of her vision.

Hmmm, I thought, I have got a problem here.

When I got home, Adele asked how things had gone.

"What I'm really dreading," I said at the conclusion of my recitation, "is when Harlene suggests we get together to try and work through our differences."

Three nights later, in the sixth inning of the third game of the Cardinals-Twins World Series, the phone rang. It was Harlene. "I've decided things can't go on like this. I'm withdrawing from the group."

"But that's not fair," I said. "It's *your* group. Can't we get together and work out our differences?" — and immediately bit my tongue.

"That won't be necessary. Daphne is withdrawing with me. I don't know Arnold's plans. Why don't you call him?"

I did not call Arnold. I completed my novel. I sent into the agent who had placed my first novel a decade earlier. "Depressing, repellant, morbid, and grim," was her judgment. But she agreed to send it to the editor-in-chief at the publisher with whom we had previously succeeded. "The most difficult to market novel I have ever read," he echoed. I found another agent. He thought it "brilliant." But a few months — and a couple rejections later — he told me he was cutting down his client list and one of those he was pruning was me. (NOTE: Before anyone gets their expectations — or gorge — up, let me point out that this was prior to Edward St Aubyn's David Meltzer raping his five-year-old son or Bret Easton Ellis' Patrick Bateman nailing young women to his living-room floor.)

I let the novel percolate. I established myself as a writer of essay/profiles about underground or alternative cartoonists, the more offbeat the better. I published a second book, about my relationship with a disabled, homeless panhandler, that was part fiction and part not.

Then I revisited my novel. This time, I thought I might increase its marketability if I added illustrations by a noteworthy cartoonist.

My choice was Maxon Crumb, Robert's younger brother, whom I had profiled some months before. Maxon lived the life of an Indian holy man on San Francisco's Skid Row. His rituals included sleeping on a bed of nails, passing a cloth through his digestive system for self-cleansing, and sitting in a lotus position on Market Street with a beggar's bow. He was epileptic and had been arrested — and committed — for improperly touching women on public conveyances. His art featured freakish images of bullets fired through brains, fingers penetrating rectums, guns penetrating vaginas, and, in one family portrait, his late brother Charles sticking an ice pick through Maxon's head. He was the strangest person I had ever met and his judgment of my book was:

> "You are the ultimate literary aghori — the ultimate literary anger baba —You are nuts — WOW! Really ... Don't bother to send this madness to publishers. They'll be returning you the men in white, not just rejection slips. You are, most likely, giving them truly frightening dreams."

Hmmm, I thought. Not a bad jacket blurb.

But I put my manuscript away instead. I continued writing feature articles about cartoonists. I published three books about them. I retired from the practice of law. Meanwhile, Milo George, a former editor of *The Comics Journal* read my book and praised it. Ryan Standfest included a portion of it in *Black Eye*, an anthology of black humor. This portion included illustrations by Ian Huebert which set me giggling.

So my confidence revived. What follows may say something about the value of perseverance. Or, as Stanley Doone, one of the characters you are about to meet, comes to reflect, I may have been better off doing push-ups in my cell.

In any event, ladies and gentlemen, twenty-five-plus years and several drafts later ...

PART

ONE.

HINKLEY MISSED

Prologue.

The worst were the tent caterpillars.

Each summer their white nests bowed the branches of the eight apple trees in the fields behind the Community like the clottings of a pestilential snow. The nests were thick, pulpy, putrescent sacs. The nests seethed and swarmed with larvae and black filth. From the nests, the infinity of caterpillars wriggled. The heat swam in the fields. The air whimpered while the caterpillars chewed the twigs and buds and blossoms.

He would take a broomstick to the fields. He would drive it upwards, thrusting, ripping, two hands at its hilt, rising on his toes. He would gut each thick, white nest. He would jab and batter. He would jelly every unmetamorphased grub. He would stomp each mite that wiggled on the ground. He would grind them heel and toe. His sweat and joy were wondrous, his elation revelatory. The field was thick with their green ooze.

It was the task that he had chosen as his sacred and professional duty. It was his honoring of Father Dynamite. It would make his mother proud.

Father Dynamite was the Main One among the Gladiators. His mother was among the Gladiettes. He was one of the Pups. All the boys and girls were Pups. They all honored Father Dynamite for teaching them to fear nothing and of nothing be ashamed by performing their duties in a sacred and professional manner. Father Dynamite taught the Pups by placing them, nude, in twos and threes and fours, in one of the Community's hot tubs and letting them frolic. Sometimes, a Gladiator or Gladiette, or, most commonly, Father Dynamite would frolic amongst them and reveal specific things not to fear and from which not to bear shame.

After he had launched the howl which Father Dynamite had instilled in his Pups and achieved his first erasure, he had to leave the Community. No one remained to protect the apple trees, so he doused their trunks, one-by-one, with gasoline and lit a match, establishing that, for all eternity, they would be clean. By then, he had named each of the trees — Snow White and Rose Red and Miss Muffett ... — but he watched them join the enduring earth and the swirling, whirling, always reforming cosmos without pain or regret.

As he drove south, the radio in his mother's Comet remarked that a young man had shot the President. The man, whose name was Hinckley, was several years older than he; but when it came to erasures, the man's aim was inferior and his howl less strong.

"STRESS REDUCTION IS MY LIFE."

Chapter I.

DOC MORG, said the vanity plate on the yellow Seville.

The garage of the pink stucco building was below street level. The tilt of the driveway, when the car's brake was applied, thrust the vanity plate into the air like an upraised middle finger. The stucco building adjoined DaVida's Monuments. The fog condensed and trickled down the faces of the granite cherubs and marble seraphim. Moss crept up their legs. Pigeon droppings crusted their wings. The saline-fortified fog etched scars into the weeping angels' smiles.

The man who got out of the Seville wore a black-and-white houndstooth jacket, cranberry silk shirt, black crushed velvet slacks, vented sharkskin moccasins. His goatee and mustache had the depth of a paintbrush stroke. His pupils held the point-of-view of a twice-hammered, five-penny nail. Let the goddamn California Medical Association bite that, Morgan Beaujack thought, glancing at his vanity plate. They gonna sue Doctor J.? Doctor Pepper? They gonna goddamn sue Doc Starks and the Night Riders?

He would admit it. The suspension from practice had hurt. He had closed his stop-smoking clinic: "Kick Some Butts." He had cancelled his weight loss classes: "Flab-U-Loss."

He had been grossing over a hundred-thou a year just punching medical reports out of his word processor for personal injury attorneys. But the Board of Medical Quality Control had him for four unnecessary surgeries and eight surgeries billed Medi-Cal but not performed and fifty patients injured in auto accidents charged four times as much for physical therapy as patients without insurance companies paying their bills.

Morgan Beaujack believed that, if he had screamed "KKK" and "Amerika" and "Old Boys keeping wealth out of the community" long enough and loud enough, he could have ridden that through. If those two chumps had not died in surgery. Even then, he had hoped BOM-QUIC would have understood. He had been under a ton of pressure. Amethyst was busting his balls in the divorce. She wanted the house in Tiburon and the 250 SL and the vineyard in Napa and $10,000 a year for fresh goddamn gladiolas when she entertained. Not that he begrudged her. Not that her tears and oaths and ultimatums hadn't won his respect. Everyone — man, woman and goddamn beast — had to do what they had to do in order to hold onto whatever they had managed to glom their paws on. Whatever it was, it seemed too little. Whatever it was, it *was* too little when you recognized what you and every other sorry motherfucker had in store. All that goddamn stone moving in and out of DaVida's, did not let him forget that.

So he had been working *mucho* hours for the *geldt*. He had been doing *mucho* coke so he could work the hours. And he had nicked those two arteries. The same artery one week apart. It was like that joke. "How'd you chop off that finger, Stosh?" "I donno. I just touched this doohickey here to that whajamacallit there and ... Damn! There goes another one." If he had nicked those two arteries a year apart, it would have been no biggie. It was not like he was that butcher up in Sacramento, racking up a body count like Jack the Goddamn Ripper. What the hell was his name? Work? Pork? Dork? It had been in all the papers.

Morgan Beaujack had not been in any papers. It was not like he had mugged a cripple on the street. He had killed two people as a Player in the company of other Players. An unfortunate human event. A tragedy for all concerned. It was something that came with the territory. That was built into their goddamn codes. That was one piece of the risk they gambled against the greater rewards. All the Players knew it could happen to anyone. "That is why God invented malpractice insurance," another orthopedic surgeon told him. "If you have never cap-sized, you have never sailed," the chief-of-staff at the hospital said. Still, they had pulled his ticket for a year. "Six months per corpse," his lawyer, Princeton Gutkin, told him. "Not too bad, considering." They had come out of that goddamn hearing room in the state building on Golden Gate. They had closed the door for the last time on that goddamn tickey-tac, formica-top furniture and that goddamn administrative law judge with his goddamn trim-it-yourself beard and his goddamn Hush Puppies and his goddamn off-the-rack Men's Warehouse suit. Princeton had clasped him by the shoulders and looked him in the eye. "Morgan, my child, listen to me closely. Watch my lips move. For one year, you do not practice medicine.

"Three hundred sixty-five days is not the end of the world."

"Easy for you to say. You don't have my support order. Amethyst's not after your *cojones* with a cleaver." "I understand you have your obligations. You will find a way to meet them. So you can't practice medicine. You can do other things. You are a talented fellow. You are a creative person." "It's too late for me to take up oil painting, Princeton. And there is not much market any more for macrame pot holders." "Morgan, perhaps you don't remember what his Honor said. Exactly what he said. 'You.' 'Can.' 'Not.' 'Practice.' 'Medicine.'" Princeton Gutkin's smile had seemed to extend the width of his pearl-gray cashmere overcoat. His silver-threaded hair, pompadour in front, swept back on the sides, had been rinsed and trimmed, blow-dried and hot-combed with an attentiveness that would have seemed excessive had its good grooming guaranteed world peace. "So for one lousy year, whatever you do, it is not medicine."

The Muzak inside the pink stucco building backed "Long Black Veil" with "Where or When." A sign on the bulletin board said: DON'T LOOK BACK. SOMETHING MAY BE GAINING. Morgan Beaujack took the interview sheet his nurse had completed from his desk. No, not his nurse. People who practiced medicine had nurses. People who did other things had assistants. They had associates. He had "my colleague, Ms. Munch." He had kept Princeton's rule in mind. So the white jacket hanging on the coat rack was a bus boy's. The stethoscope hanging over the jacket was from Morgan, Jr.'s toy set. The framed certificates in Latin were not diplomas but passages from Caesar's *Punic Wars*.

He took off his jacket and slacks. He put on a black dashiki with a gold lion on the back. He flicked his radio to KCBS. The President, in the spirit of improved international relations, it was revealed, had given the Ayatollah Khomeni a Bible and a birthday cake. He liked the president. He liked his whole goddamn trickle-down thing. It was the balls, so long as you were the one holding the hose and someone else was being pissed on.

Whatever he was doing, it was not medicine.

§

"Dave Loudermilk? Princeton Gutkin. Feeling generous today?"

"Christ. Still trying to peddle that Pagano dog? I thought I heard barking when I picked up the phone."

"Can I help it if Willie Rothstein, DDS, is trying to put his grandchildren through Stanford on my account?"

"Tell me about it. You should see my desk. You want a client with a nervous breakdown? Here I am: 'Mr. Cumulative Strain.'"

"I'll sign you up the next time you buy lunch. Seriously, David, what can you do for me on this baby?"

"God's truth, Princeton, I've known you too long to dick around. I can't go over twelve-five, no b.s."

"Excuse me? I must have a bad connection. The medical bills alone run sixty-five hundred."

"Thank you for bringing laughter into my gloomy day. Two grand for massages at Ecstasy Palace? Another thousand for hot tubs at Shangri-La Central? I'd've figured Guido for being too limp to hobble down to his chiropractor, who, incidentally, ran up twenty-five hundred for manipulations."

"Do not knock the healing arts. Your own doctor accepted the validity of the complaints, and Charles J. Wong is not exactly Marcus Welby."

"Charlie must've smoked his lunch. It's all subjectives. You try to hang two year's lost wages on that, and a jury'll bury you."

"My client showed you the letter from Tuff-Sur Freight. He earned ten-fifty an hour."

"He showed me a piece of paper a six-year-old could've typed. What he didn't was W-2s, pay check stubs or payroll records like I wanted."

"So Guido's basement flooded. So Tuff-Sur had a fire in accounting. Disasters sometimes happen."

"Princeton, Princeton ... If wishes were horses, ya-dada, ya-da."

"But if I can't beat twelve-five in court, I should turn in my copy of *Belli on Damages*. David, listen, this is one hard-nosed Sicilian. Plus, I have costs you won't believe coming out of his end. With my forty percent, he won't clear his out-of-pocket. The man will not consider a cent under fifteen clear to him, no way, not one penny."

"You are talking twenty-five grand, Princeton. That is science fiction. *Strike it Rich* went off the air a while ago, remember. I been through this with my supervisor. To do better, I have to go to a committee."

"So? Otherwise I file and serve, and your costs and fees alone'll run you over twenty. Look, David, let's wrap this up. We both have better things to do, I'm certain."

"Princeton, listen, we go way back. I'm not promising, y'understand? But suppose I could come up with twenty. Is that something your guy'd consider?"

"Maybe. If I cut my fee and eat the costs. If you're prepared to give a little, I will. I'll tell you what. I'll try. I will ask him. That's all that I can do. I know you're doing the best you can, and I appreciate the effort."

§

"Make yourself comfortable, love" Morgan Beaujack said.

"Is kind of you for see me." Mrs. Dzonot was five-foot-five. She weighed 208 pounds. She had black hair and black eyes. She had a raised mole on her nose. Black hair grew from her mole and nose and across her lower lip. It would be easier, Morgan Beaujack thought, to maintain clinical detachment if she did not look so much like Ferdinand the Bull in a goddamn dressing gown. The interview sheet said Mrs. Dzonot had been married seven years and had six children. Her old man, Jesus, was pulling two-to-five in Soledad for boosting auto parts.

Mrs. Dzonot sat on a leather-upholstered table Morgan Beaujack had bought for fifteen hundred dollars at a Castro District bath house's "Quitting Business" sale. The rest of his furniture — the cane-backed chairs, the scarlet sofa, the claw-footed lamp, the painting of the satyr and the nymphs — had not cost half that at Goodwill. It was a lesson, what you could find in San Francisco at Goodwill. The table raised and lowered electrically, all at once or in sections. In an alcove at its head, incense burned. Beside the table, in a glass vase, a sheaf of peacock feathers stood. Velvet cords were bolted to each of the table's sides. A blacksnake whip coiled at the table's foot. A purple curtain could be drawn to conceal what happened on the table.

"It says here, you suffer from stress."

"Much es-stress."

"And headaches."

"Many headachings."

"Nervousness."

"Great nervous-esness."

"And loss of appetite."

"All day. All night. Headachings. Nervous-esness. No appetites." Mrs. Dzonot looked like she expected to be tossed a biscuit for how well she had performed. "Sometimes, I think I never be well."

"The classic signs." He rapped her scapula with two fingers. "Serious, love, if true." Mrs. Dzonot winced — and smiled.

Morgan Beaujack tapped her patella.

Mrs. Dzonot grimaced — and batted her eyes.

"Open wide and say, 'Ahhh.'"

"Ahhhhhh! Doc-tor Morg, you can help me?"

"Stress reduction is my life." He had removed one of her shoes. He was massaging her foot. "But sound health is a partnership. We must work together, body and soul."

"I have heard habout your es-special treatments. Your fan-dastic services. Is possible I may be hanother worthy candidate?" "It is not out of the question." He had scuffled, but he would last the year. The news was out about Doc Morg and his Miracle Cure. It traveled on a network of old ladies and widows and divorcees. It passed along the wire of the lost, the damaged, the alone. The people who had given up on singles bars and classified ads and the second cousins of good-old Liz in the typing pool. The ones who had recognized hope as a yowling cat, at three a.m., cutting through the Seconal and Cutty. Who knew desire was a pustule to lance before it festered. Who had attained the clarity to recognize that every itch deserved its scratch.

Morgan Beaujack knew. He understood. He recognized the ease with which all yearnings happened. Morgan Beaujack did not blame. He did not accuse. He would not cast the inaugural stone. He embraced the opportunity offered. He believed himself blessed by the chance to fill the void.

And it was goddamn happening. You could not beat the word of mouth for publicity. A few more happy customers and he might tell the C.M.A. to keep his goddamn license. Who needed the hassles and the overhead? The dues and insurance? The small minded bureaucrats afraid of the new? He was not sure he was not relieving more pain than when he was in practice. He had his days, like his daddy used to say, as happy as the sissy in the troop train. He had only to overcome one or two of his own discriminatory hang-ups, and he could double his market share. He was massaging her ankle, and she was breathing hard.

"It depends on the depth of the problem." Morgan Beaujack shut the purple curtain. He hiked the dressing gown around Mrs. Dzonot's thighs and drew her lilac panties down. "Just lie back and relax. Spread your legs. Place one arm here. And here." He tied her wrists with the velvet cords. He selected a peacock feather. "We must test some neuro-anatomical responses. A deep breath, please."

"Oh."

"Does it hurt there?"

"OH!"

"There?"

"OHH!"

"Count backwards from 100 by nine."

"OHHH! OHHH! OHHH!"

Morgan Beaujack returned the feather to the vase. He hesitated for a moment to compose his features, modulate his tone, engage the catch within his throat — to knit the bolt between authority and complicity that the masquerade required for dignity and grace to be afforded. He had chosen his profession not entirely because he foresaw it ending in a vineyard. There had been the idea of aid and comfort and the easing of mortifications. He had used his skills and expertise, his education and his manner. He had prescribed and advised, palpated and probed and, if appropriate, knelt side-by-side in prayer. He had lain on hands when they were indicated, and he saw no reason now to hold back any other solace-providing appendage. The benefits of the Placebo Effect were well-documented in journals. It was not only sugar pills that succored. In his way, he was not without standards or compassion. "I'm afraid, love, my worst fears are true."

"No," Mrs. Dzonot said.

"There is no denying the symptoms. Heart pounding ..."

She nodded.

"... shortness of breath ..."

She nodded again.

"... flushed complexion. My diagnosis must be FRAIDS. Female Reverse Auto-Immune Disease Syndrome. As you may have heard, there is only one known cure. Intimate relations with a certified antibody bearer. Intimate relations with ... me."

"Doc-tor Morg, it is God's will. I will be brave."

"You may need multiple sessions."

"Quick, please, do not waste one second."

§

"Ten thousand don't sound like a lot, Mr. Gutkin, for the hell what I been through." "Facts are facts, Guido. Your case, to use the vernacular, ain't worth shit. You know that as well as me." "My neck. My back. My doctor can't find what's wrong. You telling me my pain and suffering's worth nothing?" "That is *your* doctor. Your nephew, the doctor. I'm surprised that moron can find his fly to stick his dong back when he whizzes. The insurance company's doctor — a regular Mayo brother — compares you favorably to Conan the Barbarian." "It's my fault sometimes I have a good day? I been off work two years. You show them my letter." "And I did not point out the return address is your sister Frannie's, who, last time I looked, did not have a loading dock out back. Besides, between Mutual of Dubuque and Social Security, you're bringing home eighty percent of your best year." "But ten-thou ain't no money. You take your third, and nothing's left for me." "If I took a third, two-thirds would be left you. But I take forty. Plus expenses. And don't suggest I cut my fee. Contracts are a sacred trust on which the fabric of a civilized society depends." "I donno. It's a big decision. Maybe I ought to talk it over with the wife. Maybe get a second opinion." "You can never be too careful. Of course, you see another attorney, he'll charge you for his time. And while you futz around, the money could be working for you. Guido, Guido, Guido, you hired me, didn't you? Nobody twisted your arm. You should respect the advice I give you." "But ten thousand dollars? They expect me to live on that? They want me to rob a bank?" "Client I had tried that. They nailed him before he hit East 80. Within the week, three jigs in County had Tommy's behind as their personal sperm bank. Suppose I could get twelve-five?" "You think they'd go for that?"

"I'd make every effort. I believe in you, Guido. You know that. I've got some strings left to pull." "I'd clear what ... seventy-five. I don't want them to think I'm nickel-diming, but how 'bout you try and squeeze a little more." "Thirteen thousand do it? I want to know I can make a deal. I don't like running back and forth. Insurance companies have to know they can trust me in negotiations. I have my reputation." "New money?"

"New money."

"Tax free?"

"Absolutely?"

"They pay thirteen thousand, they can forget they ever knew me."

§

"Your two o'clock is here."

"In a minute."

"Is the client Herr Gutkin vanted you examine." Inge Munch helped Morgan Beaujack out of his dashiki. She handed him the white jacket. "You reviewed his records yesterday."

"Oh yeah. Goddamn tricky business, hernia repair."

Inge Munch straightened a stack of *People* magazines. She aligned the cane-backed chairs. Her red hair was pinned atop her head. She wore black, calf-length boots. Two buttons on her green dress were open at the throat. "Frau Dzonot seemed to be feeling better ven she left."

"That is gratifying to hear."

"She request three appointments next veek."

"Well, well, well."

"She ask if you could sqveeze her sister in."

"At the same time?"

"Separate. At least, at first, I vould imagine."

"I suppose I can give family special consideration."

"I took the liberty of Tuesday at five-sirty."

"Fine. And re-order peacock feathers. These are frayed."

"Is a pleasure, Herr Doctor, to vork mitt someone so concerned mitt patients' vell-being." "I like to think I've got my priorities screwed tight. By the way ..." "Bank account in order. Credit card mitt ample limits."

"Darling, your way of anticipating needs is positively outstanding." "Anything to lighten your load. Sometime ..." Inge Munch licked her lips. "... I vorry you drive yourself too hard." "It has been a long day." Morgan Beaujack pictured the sculpture standing in rows in the adjoining yard in rows like punished children who would not be permitted shelter until they confessed their sins. He could feel the wind and fog lacerating the granite. He could hear the angels scream. "I could do with some stress reduction myself. To tell you the truth ..." He glanced at the leather table. "... I have been naughty." "I see." Inge Munch's eyebrows seized into a configuration as formidable as the Siegfried Line. Her lips lay stiff as riot batons.

"Very naughty."

"You know vot happens to naughty boys?"

Morgan Beaujack nodded.

"To very naughty boys?"

He nodded again.

"Den, for vot are we vaiting?" Inge Munch led Morgan Beaujack to the leather table. She picked up the blacksnake whip. Then, she spoke, as if of something she was frightened to forget. "Sis client of Herr Gutkin ... He seemed ... vell, ... strange."

Strange, Morgan Beaujack thought, unbuckling his trousers, exposing his buttocks and bending forward. What in this world could be strange?

Haven

Chapter II.

The Law Offices of Princeton Gutkin occupied the ground floor of a restored warehouse, north of Jackson Square. The brick building had once housed Kutler Bros. Meats. Now file cabinets full of rear-enders, slip-and-falls, excavation site collapses stood where the headless, hideless carcasses had hung. Now Bally loafers stepped where viscous drippings had soaked the sawdust red. Gutkin was a personal injury attorney, whose livelihood depended on others' shattered bones and severed tendons, their fractured skulls and shredded dreams, their lullabies grown into screams. Despite the parallels in carnage, he had made the premises his own.

His secretary, Panda, hair and eyes as black as pitch, perched in a Polynesian sarong behind an eighteenth century mahogany bar salvaged from the ballroom of a China clipper. A rain forest of tree ferns oxygenated the reception area. A charm of finches chirped from bamboo cages, while hidden speakers played Tito, Mongo, Martin Denny. Beside each rattan chair, a *faux* pirate's chest over-flowed with gold foil-wrapped, chocolate doubloons. The walls displayed the heads of a lion, tiger, leopard and hyena beside the Mannlichers that had apparently slain them.

Princeton Gutkin knew it was a little Hollywood, but, hey, he knew his clients too. They were like anybody else: HURT and MAD. They wanted two things: MONEY and REVENGE. His waiting room declared that they were more likely to get that here than from any white-shoe firm on Montgomery Street. "This man BAD," the mounted heads snarled. "He offed us beasts. He be REAL BAD for you." "This man live FINE," the chocolates jingled. "He make BIG BUCKS. He make PLENTY for you." The fact that the trophies came from an estate sale in Cupertino and that the confectioner's bill was already in collection did not keep Gutkin's message from singing more hypnotically than his sound system's sambas.

Princeton Gutkin's private office sent a message too. Like the Blackfoot brave who ate the grizzly's heart to absorb its power, he incorporated within its walls the most ferocious instruments to have mauled his clients. The tire that exploded when Melinda Muffett's Audi came around Wildcat Curve. The ladder which snapped when R. B. Wimsey reached for his satellite dish. The glass panel through which Mimi Schenck walked at her gallery opening. The dress which combusted when Lorelai Ono received her duck flambé. The Coca-Cola sign that fell on Wendell Klinger as he returned from the bishop's installation. Each day that Gutkin maneuvered by these macabre souvenirs without snagging one thread of his Brioni suit reinforced his belief that his life was charmed. And the framed photographs of him handing clients checks reminded him of the bullion that could be mined from blood.

Princeton Gutkin knew some people saw more in the law than bullion. They had this idea about perfection. This idea that law could order society to achieve justice for man. That idea was wild. Here was man, this flux, this clash, this sweep and surge, unpredictable, uncontainable, capable of so many actions: DRIVING CARS; LIGHTING FIRES; ACQUIRING BEDROOM SUITES; FRANCHISING ROAST BEEF SANDWICH OUTLETS; HUGGING AND SCHTUPPING; GIVING AND TAKING LIFE. And here was the law, static, rigid, frozen blocks of black against the white page, products of other men — legislators — who studied, researched, debated, and set down precisely who could DRIVE CARS, how old, how sighted, at what speed, on which road, with how many horns or lights — considerations to make the drive of all men optimal. And the legislators did the same for BEDROOM SUITES and SCHTUPPING and SHOOTING MOOSE and SHOOTING EACH OTHER. And other men — judges — read the words, heard arguments, and considered phrases and comma placements and the intent of legislators, often long dead, to declare what the words meant, not uncommonly coming to conclusions opposite to what most men and other judges had, until then, believed, causing each SHOOTER and SCHTUPPER to shift his own conduct to follow these new meanings toward reperceived perfection.

The process seemed more noble than mad only as long as you believed in logical, ordered progress toward perfectible, attainable justice. And Princeton Gutkin's consciousness had accumulated, like tissue toxic poison, too many illogical, unjust failed brakes, slips on lettuce leaves, and exploding hair dryers for that. There were mornings when his mirror showed him a creature that cheered train derailments and booed miraculous recoveries. That applauded multi-vehicular wrecks and hissed medical breakthroughs. There were evenings when he felt like a ghoul, crouched in the weeds for another corpse to pounce on.

But hey, Princeton Gutkin would tell himself, don't overdo the self-condemnation. Grocers feed off others' hunger. Disease launches physicians on Aegean cruises. If people were not scared of the dark, the Pope himself would be sleeping on the Spanish Steps. The world will always mutilate. Why should there be no money in it? And who can say Bobo Grabowski was not better off with the fifty thousand he'd cleared than with his left foot, which was only bringing home two hundred dollars a week in flush times? Maybe that was Bobo's jackpot. His winning spin on fortune's wheel. Maybe, now, he sends a kid to Harvard; and the kid discovers a cure for cancer, meaning his attorney, whose Request for Documents blew the case wide open, will have made more of a social contribution than if he had gone into fighting for due process with the A.C.L.U.

So, normally, when sitting at his captain's desk, Princeton Gutkin smiled.

Princeton Gutkin frowned and tried to recall this Heavens he had sent for medical evaluation.

"I've reviewed the records," Morgan Beaujack said, tapping an index finger on the Red Robe file. "Esubio Chabchap may not be the slickest surgeon in town, but I don't see anything he did wrong when he cut into this character."

"Not to worry, Morg. Med mal's no guaranteed gold goose these days. You docs have been weeping about insurance premiums so long, juries perform like rooting sections for you more than deliberative bodies. Even if you'd made me out a *prima facie*, I might've punted."

"The op report, lab tests, nurses' notes — it all washes clean. Plus, you tie up a fortune in costs, pending resolution." A human skeleton, Pritikin, his courtroom visual aide, dangled from Princeton Gutkin's ceiling. He pushed a foot and heard ribs rattle, tibia clap against fibula, ulna on radius, mortality transmute to music, chiller to cartoon. *Thank you*, began the dictation in his head, *For the confidence expressed in this office by consulting me about your claim.*

"But something bothers me more than you not proving liability." "His check bounced ... I'll cover it." *However, my investigation reveals I would be unlikely to prosecute it successfully on your behalf.*

"What do you know about your client?"

Princeton Gutkin had been referring Morgan Beaujack patients for years. For an early birthday present, Morgan would prescribe enough physical therapy to quadruple the value of any sore neck. A pair of Niners tickets brought narrative reports that made scraped elbows sound like the eleventh plague. True, the suspension of his license had reduced Morgan's usefulness. You could not waltz him into court to testify to the ruin some *de minimis* impact had bestowed. But his not being able to bill as much for his time made him a fine choice to screen a possible malpractice action. Morgan had been around, and the tone of his question suggested to Gutkin that he leave out *Feel free to call upon me again.*

"Not much," Princeton Gutkin said. "Big fellow. Ran a forklift for Kwilty-Humberg. Quiet. Pissed. Scar like somebody tried to bite off half his nose. Not exactly Disney Channel material, you know what I mean?" Morgan Beaujack did not smile. "He said since his operation he'd been hurting. What the hell, I figured. Maybe some stoned resident left his roach clip inside. Maybe they misread the blueprint and stuck his gall bladder where his pee-pee should be. I got a release for his records and sent him and them to you to see if we could shake out some shekels for the good guys."

"Well, you sure landed one purple-assed mofo." All Morgan Beaujack's fingers were tapping now. "His presenting complaints were so off the goddamn wall — stinging nipples, burning *pipick*, a ticker that wheezed and fluttered and damn near whistled *Hello, Dolly* — he must of taken the glaze in my eyes for tears of sympathy. The hairball decided to level with me. And it seems your Mr. Heavens is convinced my man Esubio plugged him with a goddamn computer chip, programmed to cause him grief."

"Schizzy City, huh?" Princeton Gutkin sliced open the last envelope in his mail. "FINAL WARNING," the bill from Pickwick Court Reporting said. It had been that kind of day. His ten o'clock new client had cancelled without rescheduling. The police report had showed no negligence on the motorcycle that clipped the Limerick girl. Elmo Pepp's blood alcohol had been double the legal limit when he stepped in front of the Veteran's Cab. Now Jerome Heavens had proved another dry hole.

That's not all." Morgan Beaujack shook his head. "He wants to off the good doctor's sorry ass." Princeton Gutkin put down his letter opener. He rose from his chair and walked to the window. A dead fly lay on the sill, legs stuck in the air as if it was joking.

"The phenomenon is not uncommon. Surgeries are major traumas. Weakly balanced egos may not withstand the strain. Marginal people sometimes crumble. But, Princeton, I have seen a lot of crazies, and this cat is the scariest."

"Did my ... Are we ... Any other names come up in the conversation?"

"Negative."

"Well ..."

"I already warned brother Chabchap. The dude almost shit. I suggested he close up shop, drop from sight, witness pro-tec-tion-ate the entire *meshpucha*, take a long vacation."

"Can't the man be treated?"

"He won't voluntarily see anyone. He doesn't think it's him with the problem. If he succeeds in snuffing Chabchap, he figures he'll be *Time*'s 'Man of the Year,' for eliminating a threat to Western Civilization as we know it." Morgan Beaujack mopped his brow with a midnight blue handkerchief. "And involuntary commitment's too risky. They can't 5150 him forever. When he gets out, the only change will be more names on his Enemies List."

Princeton Gutkin looked at the chain of stalled cars and angry drivers clogging Broadway, from the Columbus Avenue tunnel to the Embarcadero. The exhaust from the cars fouled the air. The anger of the drivers fouled their veins. The cars and drivers were trying to honk and bully their way to places they were not. Behind them, other cars and drivers honked and bullied for the spots these cars and drivers held. Stretched across the city, through every boulevard and alley, up and down its seven hills, chains of cars and drivers strangled it. Every morning, the horror started earlier. Every evening, it lasted longer. Soon, to be on time for your spot in Thursday's traffic, you would have to leave your office Tuesday noon. "Calm down, Morgan. Let me get you some chablis."

"I'm telling you, all we can do is wait and hope. Hope he never gets to the point he acts. Hope he's pancaked by a steamroller. These are goddamn scary motherfuckers, Princeton. We don't know much about them. Right now, the only person threatened is Chabchap. No one else is encompassed by the delusional system. That doesn't mean they won't be. Friend Heavens may go on normally for years and, one morning, wipe out Little Sisters of the Poor."

The alarm on a Taurus wailed like it had been gored. A Kawasaki, climbing Stockton, shrieked against the grade. Princeton Gutkin felt his heart pound and his temples throb as if some inner spirit wished to beat its way free of the confinement of the human condition. He was used to a world where innocent people were randomly felled by speeding cars, spilled baby oil, and splintering chair legs, without regard to age or sex or extent of charitable contributions. These events were frightening but chance. They shrank in comparison to this crazed hunter, stalking vengeance for a hallucinated wrong. If your fate depended on chance, you could take precautions, avoid risks, lengthen odds, check speedometers, watch where you walked or sat. Destruction that targeted and tracked, based upon the reasoned plottings of the idiot-insane, shook him at his core.

But hey, Princeton Gutkin reminded himself. You are an attorney. You have been educated to treat all facts as potential weapons. You have been trained to view all principles as negotiable ground. You have a prime legal mind: ORDERED; LOGICAL. One that can DISTINGUISH, as well as CONNECT. It is an attribute of the prime legal mind to be dispassionate; and hey, you can do that. The shock from the revelation of Heavens' nature began to dissipate. He could treat it like any other information: WEIGH IT; CLASSIFY IT; STICK IT IN THE FREEZER, where it would keep for future use. He did not know what that might be, but hey, anything could happen.

Panda brought the carafe and glasses from the coffee room. She set down the tray and left, hair swaying, hips twitching. "I trust domestic will do," Princeton Gutkin said.

"Right now," Morgan Beaujack said, "Wet is good enough for me."

Chapter III.

"You guys don't have mice," Rudy from Borgia Services said. "You got rats."

"Rats!" Princeton Gutkin said.

"Tubular!" Tisa Rio said.

They were in the living room. Tisa Rio sat in a full lotus on the nappy white sofa that slunk along three walls. Princeton Gutkin leaned against his eight-by-ten, cherry veneer home-entertainment system: rear-projector big screen TV, compact disc with Dolby; VHS and Beta. Rudy stood under the LeRoy Neiman oil of Gutkin haranguing a judge. Rudy held a Mylar envelope with pellets, black like bee-bees.

"You got any idea what this place cost me?" Princeton Gutkin said. "An arm and a leg. Lit'rally. Angel Weintraub's arm. Willie Binns' leg. And you're saying I got rats?"

"Everybody's got rats. Queen of England. Sylvester Stallone. It don't make no difference. Bastards're everywhere." "They're too short to reach the elevator buttons," Tisa Rio said. "What, they hike up sixteen floors?" "Bastards go for where the food is. Grow wings if they have to. You got to hand it to the bastards. They get where they want to go." "Outside of admiring Mother Nature," Princeton Gutkin said, "how you suggest we remedy the situation?" "Deed's already done. Laid poison at your primary access locations. I just hope you guys don't have pets or kids. And I hope youse don't sleep nibble. 'Cause this shit is lethal. The beauty of it's how it prays on the nature of the beast. See, just 'cause it kills one rat don't mean it quits working. Other rats'll eat the dead one, and it'll poison them. Rats, like man, been known to eat each other."

After dinner, Princeton Gutkin liked to stand on his balcony and flick the ash from his Monte Christo at the lights of the city, sparkling gold and silver, ruby and emerald, at his pedicured feet. It had been a long haul from his family's shotgun apartment, South-o'-the-Slot, to the top of the tallest condo on Cathedral Hill. For his monthly payment, he figured, hey, he could crap over the rail.

Princeton Gutkin had made the satisfaction of his desires the center of his life. So the world was brutal. He would use the profits from its havoc to spin a cocoon — rose-scented, silk-swathed, chocolate-dipped — that would warm and nourish him. He had the superstar trial attorney's gifts: DRIVE; DETERMINATION; SELF-CONFIDENCE as devoid of natural enemies as the great white shark. In his view, everybody else walked two steps behind, emptying ashtrays, dusting rubber plants, while he strode forward, grabbing lions by the scruff, tossing hammers back and forth with Thor. No consideration, whether as small as an opponent's case or as great as repercussions for society as a whole, made him doubt a client's right to triumph or his own.

But this evening he slouched in an Eames chair, his cigar dead between his lips. The fact was, he was in bad financial shape. In the past year, he had lost three jury trials. Since he had the cases on a contingency, not only had he pocketed no fees, he was out the three hundred thousand he had advanced in costs. The trials had taken so long, tying him up for six months, three other blue chip clients had quit him; and he had been too busy to bring others in.

It would have been better, he thought, to have flushed the three hundred-K down the toilet. At least, then, people would not have read he lost three trials. Then four more clients would not have walked, thinking him over the hill. Then defendants would not be refusing to settle, figuring he could not afford to go to trial and would cut his price. Bread-and-butter cases, like Guido Pagano's, were fine. They kept gas in the Carrera. But they did not get it for you in the first place. To get the Porsche and the penthouse and the Nieman, you needed two, three, four big scores a year. This year, he had not scored. This year, they had handed him his rear. It was always feast or famine in P.I. You did the same work on the big case as the small. You took the same depositions; you answered the same interrogatories. Sometimes, you worked your nuts off and got *bupkis*. Sometimes, you scratched one ball and walked off with a quarter-mill.

Always, before, it evened out. Always, before, the big cases came through. This year, though, was something else. This year, the probabilities broke down. This year, some place, some night, some guy had dreamed about the seven starving cows; and he, Princeton Gutkin, had not got the news. Maybe "bad" was not the word for his financial situation. Maybe the word was that, when Panda told him they needed toilet paper for the john, he told her to cop a roll from Burger King.

With problems like that, who needed Morgan Beaujack's homicidal Loony Toon messing with his mind?

"What's the matter?" Tisa Rio said.

"Nothing."

"Keeping secrets, hon, 's not nice."

"I told you, baby. Nothing is the matter."

"'Nothing is the matter.' Right." Tisa Rio's honey-blond hair was woven into a French braid. She wore a pair of stonewashed 401's, cut off at the crotch, and a "Follow Your Bliss" t-shirt bought one adjective too small. "That's how come you look like you're auditioning for a Preparation H commercial."

"Can't a guy think without you acting like he's plotting to take out Mother Teresa?" "Dr. Chumus says intimacy is the key to a successful relationship. 'For intimacy to happen, communication must be open and clear,' Dr. Chumus says." "Chumus is a furry, four-eyed chump. For one twenty-five a pop, you'd think he could afford to get his natural fibers cleaned. How come you keep seeing him? Whatever happened to that ..." Princeton Gutkin fluttered a hand in front of his mouth. "... Woo-woo! — Injun, the one that had us rolling on the floor to lose our inhibitions? I loosed my inhibitions, all right. The time he grabbed my rod." "For Baba Doya, unrestrained sensuality was the key for fully released chakra." "Terrific. My chakra was sore for two days. But the swami was cool. White robes. Purple turban. Handlebar 'stash. Not like Chumus, with his Woodstock-issue Birkenstocks, Abbie Hoffman 'do, and Mr. Natural beaver. At least, you could take the swami someplace. Looking at his threads wouldn't tell you what he had for Wednesday's lunch." "You must quit being judgmental, hon, and recognize all people's purity of spirit. Besides, 'Sticks and stones ...'" Tisa Rio caught herself. Maintaining contact with her inner child had been central to her work with Ramae Skye Foxe, but Dr. Chumus insisted that her adult persona needed to emerge. Seize the power; recognize your entitlement, he told her. Empowerment was her goal. "Besides, the subject isn't my path to spiritual fulfillment. Or the table manners of the people I meet on my way. The subject is our level of communication. Or lack of it, I might say." "Well, ex-cuuuuse me. What's on my mind is business. The business that gets your Dr. Chumus paid." "Which reminds me ..."

"And your astrologer. And palm reader ..."

"... he says we owe him ..."

"... polarity therapist, iridiologist, and your nitwit Breema body works mechanic." "... for the last three months."

"But do you ever want to talk about business? About what is important to me?" Princeton Gutkin stood up. "No, business is 'Boring.' Business is 'Disgusting.' All you want to talk about is auras and karmas and out-of-body experiences. You keep bugging me, Tisa; and I'll give you out-of-body experiences." He windmilled his right arm. "POW!"

"I am willing to hear about your business, hon. Anything important to you is important to me. That is what I'm trying to tell you. Sharing is the crux of a good relationship, Dr Chumus says. Just treat me as a partner. Respect my mind and being."

"Partners. Mind and being. Got it. Swell. Anything else? Should I take notes or just begin?" "I could do with a scosh less sarcasm too."

"One scosh. Yes, ma'am. Well, here is some of my business. Here is how I capped my day. Watched two hours of film some jerk-off investigator from Doberman Indemnity shot of Mrs. Heinz. The clown sat outside her house for three weeks, seven days a week, ten hours a day to prove her back was healed. Every time she came outside, Sam Spade took movies. You know what he got? Three weeks? Ten hours a day? Mrs. Heinz getting in her car. Mrs Heinz driving to Stonestown. Mrs. Heinz getting out of her car. Mrs. Heinz walking to the mall. Mrs. Heinz coming out. Mrs. Heinz getting in her car. Mrs. Heinz driving home. Mrs. Heinz getting in her car the next day. Mrs. Heinz driving to Stonestown. In the same blue coat. In the same blue dress. With the same dumb look on her same dumb face. Three entire weeks. I wanted to give him an Oscar when he finally got her hosing her lawn. Know what two hours watching Mrs. Heinz was like?"

Tisa Rio shook her head.

"The worst. Like watching one of those Andy Warhol movies you hear about, except, instead of some schmuck sleeping, you got Mrs. Heinz driving to the mall." Princeton Gutkin picked up his cigar, then put it down, then picked it up again. "After the first thirty minutes, I was asking myself, 'Is that Mrs. Heinz's life? Driving to Stonestown?' After an hour, I was asking, 'What if some investigator was filming me?' What would he be showing except two hours of Princeton Gutkin driving to his office, driving fucking home. I got it so much better than goofy Mrs. Heinz?'"

"Your life would be a love-fest, if you opened to each moment." "Know what roses tomorrow offers me to smell? Answering eighty pages of interrogatories sent to Louis Glanz. 'Name every place you ever lived.' 'Give the name, address and date of visit to every doctor you ever saw.' 'Tell every job you ever held, your rate of pay, the reason you left, and where its men's room is located.' Guess what going through that's like with a seventy-year-old, got an IQ of twelve." "Boring?"

"'Name every place you ever farted.' 'How many times you wipe when you shit?' 'With how many sheets of what color Charman?'"

"Dis-GUST-ing." Tisa Rio flung a hand to her mouth. "You made that up. To get me to say 'Boring' and 'Disgusting.' So you wouldn't have to talk to me." She flounced from the room, the loose threads of her 401s rippling against her thighs.

Princeton Gutkin was sorry to see her go. In their six years together, Tisa had become a central pillar in his palace of pleasure. When he first saw her, that was not the program. She was dangling from a cable car by one hand, thwacked on X, squirting champagne from a magnum on the Datsun she was passing. Tisa was nineteen, wore purple suede boots, black leotard, crimson halter top, had that honey-colored hair swinging to her asshole. She had been in town ten months from Sulfleur Pond, New Jersey. She was working as a masseuse in the Tenderloin. Before that, she had waitressed at a Mission cocktail lounge, modeled for live-drawing at the Art Institute, bartended topless in North Beach, all the while studying trans-channeling and astral plane projection and third-eye expansion with any guru had a prayer mat he could call his own. He had chased her half way up Nob Hill, figuring she was one more gold ring to grab and toss when he was done.

But Tisa, it turned out, was good for more than slap-and-tickle. She was fresh. She was fun. She had this trick with crushed ice and Readi-Whip. Having something steady to come home to was all right. He did not even mind her spacey side. Whacking off Jap businessmen might not make her Commonwealth Club material; but he could get behind her being independent, having a career. So long as her chanting and floor rolling did not bruise her exterior, Tisa adding depth might be a good thing. It would not hurt his public image to have a significant other whose library was not limited to *X-Men*, like some bimbos he had known. Whose Saturday mornings were not inviolate because of Roadrunner cartoons. Maybe he was, after all, a closet woman's lib-type guy. And, hey, you never knew when some tofu-head from one of her ashrams might fall into a cement mixer and need a good attorney. One good leg-off would pay for a lot of workshops on dreams.

The problem was that, when they met, Tisa had the small town girl's limited view; but once inside his penthouse, her horizons had expanded. Now, one silver Porsche was no longer sufficient. For when it was in the shop, an equally loaded alternate was required. Now, two weeks on Maui, in December, could not be expected to hold together body and soul an entire winter. Not when rain could fall in January, February, March, and Bali, Bimini, and Bora-Bora had sunny beaches on which to scamper.

When he was well-off, he enjoyed satisfying Tisa. But each month his credit card statements read more like scrolls, he worried she would leave. No skirt had ever booked on him before, but he knew it could happen. A new world was out there. Twists he knew had gone gay or Christian or had so many piercings a porcupine made better cuddling. And don't even mention HIV. Hey, don't even think it. It did not count any more with broads that he had represented Huey Newton for a dog bite. That, in 1980, he got loaded with Bill Graham at Perry's. Each morning, it took longer, with spray and brush, to cover his bald spot. Each year, his belt slipped out another notch, no matter how many laps he schlogged in the club pool or how much *schvitz* he swallowed. In the past, he would repeatedly dream he had flunked Tax I, never graduated Golden Gate, had his whole career eradicated. Now it was that Tisa had split and he had to start dating.

"Boo!" Tisa Rio had removed her t-shirt and jeans. The ice bag was in one hand and the Readi-Whip on his favorite places. Another admirable quality, Princeton Gutkin thought, was her inability to hold a grudge.

Before he made a move, the telephone rang. Princeton Gutkin looked at Tisa. He looked at the phone. What Tisa offered was top drawer. But the office line was on call-forwarding, and it could be anything.

"Hope I'm not interrupting, counselor," Chickie Gilligan said.

Princeton Gutkin &
Stanley Doone

Chapter IV.

Mt. Bilbo Hospital's cafeteria was in the basement, close enough to the laundry to have the odor of dirty sheets pinned forever on its air. Princeton Gutkin moved his tray down the line, trying to keep breathing to a minimum. Flies flitted amidst the jello. The salads resembled a series of still lives in brown. He settled for a package of Ritz crackers. He poured coffee into an ocher cup with a crack from base to brim.

At one table, a psychiatric technician was shredding *USA Today* into a thousand pieces. At a second, two radiologists were exchanging confidences about backhand grips and no-load mutual funds. At a third, one inhalation therapist was describing to another the joy of double-headed dildos.

"Glad you could make it." Chickie Gilligan sat against the back wall. His grimy felt hat was pulled down to his eyes. He had not shaved in three days. He was missing two lower front teeth. Chickie's grey wool worsted looked like it had been special ordered from *Rag Pickers' Daily* and smelled like a fifty-fifty blend of Camel butts and Rainier Ale.

"Chickie, I come in here, considering what's on the steam table, honest to God, I'm not sure I haven't stumbled into Pathology by mistake."

"In Pathology, less of the company sits up."

Princeton Gutkin tore open the cellophane wrapper. The first cracker he touched crumbled to dust.

"Nice talent," Chickie Gilligan said.

"I'd do gold. But it means *tsouris* with the I.R.S." The coffee was cold and reminded him of socks after eight hours wear. "This better be good. You made me miss dessert."

"Six weeks intensive care sound better than cherry pie?" Chickie Gilligan salted his fried egg sandwich with one hand. He peppered with the other. Then he held the ketchup bottle upside down and socked the bottom.

Chickie Gilligan had been a five-star San Francisco trial attorney until he was disbarred after being caught in bed with the forewomen on the jury of a Murder One he was trying. Everybody had their favorite

Chickie story. Princeton Gutkin liked the time Chickie was defending this Samoan charged with murdering his wife. The district attorney had them arguing. He had a bloody hatchet. He had the Samoan wiping out the joint savings the day she disappeared and flying to Cozatmul. He didn't have a body though. At the start of the D.A.'s summation, U.P.S. Wheeled a trunk into the courtroom. All the time the D.A. was arguing, the jury was staring at that trunk, padlocked and chained. The D.A. went on and on. "The People's case is solid. Circumstantial evidence compels conviction. The absence of the body's unimportant. The body doesn't mean a thing." No one on the jury was hearing a word. All of a sudden, Chickie shouted, "Oh yeah"; and out of the trunk hopped Carol Doda.

Now Chickie was over seventy. He had a bad liver and a bad heart. He could not see out of his right eye or hear out of his left ear. Princeton Gutkin paid him by the hour to serve papers, do light research, some investigating. Gutkin liked having a half-deaf, half-blind investigator. He thought it cast a proper light on the nature of truth in litigable matters. He liked, too, that if Chickie found a case, he knew where to bring it.

"Princeton, on this one, you could make out with the Plaster of Paris account alone." Chickie Gilligan was too excited to notice the yolk dribbling down his chin.

Princeton Gutkin was not excited. He knew the biggest car crash in recorded history, occurring in the middle of your family picnic, did not guarantee you banked a dime. Every last one of your nieces and nephews could walk away without a skinned knee between them. Or their body parts could be strewn all over the lawn without it meaning the driver was to blame. Or you could prove two dozen Vehicle Code violations, and his carrier could have cancelled him that morning. Or you could hit the trifecta — DAMAGES, LIABILITY, INSURANCE — and be holding a screwball client like Mrs. Fitzwater, who refused to sue S.F. Muni because the driver who squashed her left tootsie had been nice to her Lhasa apso. Drawings — poster paint on butcher paper — by the children in Mt. Bilbo's Terminal Ward decorated the cafeteria and Gutkin tamped down Chickie Gilligan's enthusiasm by staring at the brightly colored horses, trees, and flowers of the gene-cursed kiddies.

“And nobody’s signed up Mr. Pot O’Gold? I’m not looking to get slapped with any interference-with-a-contractual-relationship-beef.”

“Lighten up, Princeton. The sky’s not falling. The docs keep this baby under lock and key.” “But you got in?”

“When you travel cross-country for one look at your only grandchild ... When your health may not permit another visit ...” “Don’t tell me. When the Assembly Sub-committee on Client Solicitation issues its subpoenas, there are things I do not need to know.” “Credibility-wise, age has its privileges. Not that I wouldn’t trade all my white hair, weathered visage, and accumulated wisdom for a stiff nine-inches of Mr. Meat.” Chickie Gilligan bent over with a hacking cough. He fanned what was left of his sandwich in front of his mouth. “And once I was alone with the injured party, I explained how I was on a fact-finding mission, commissioned by an eminent barrister already engaged in the aggressive representation of a plethora of clients run down by rampaging semi’s exactly like the one which nailed him. Just cross-checking information, I told him, for our class action. Purely a consumer oriented inquiry. Strictly Ralph Nader up the bazoo. Like 'Did the truck have its frammis bolted?' 'Was the dip stick fully race-lined?' 'By the way,' I may have mentioned, 'If you haven't yet retained counsel, my principal may have a spare moment to answer any questions on your mind.'" "Such as, 'Where do I sign my name?'"

"Said thought occurred."

Princeton Gutkin poured a stream of sugar into his cup. "So who is this guy? Mr. Opportunity Knocking?" "Stanley."

"'Stanley.' Nice, Chickie. Gentle, unpretentious, old worldly, regular guy-ish." "Stanley Doone."

"Stanley fucking-Doone taken any vows of poverty I should know about? Any *meshugana* renouncements of all interest in worldly goods? Forgive my cautious nature."

"Six weeks intensive care, old buddy. You won't know how to thank me." Princeton Gutkin stirred his coffee. "Okay, Chickie. This works out, I'll take care of you Christmas." "Princeton, this time, if you should remember me Groundhog's Day and Simchas Torah besides, it won't hurt."

To ease Princeton Gutkin's passage through Mt. Bilbo, Chickie Gilligan had hung a beeper on his belt, stuck a tongue depressor in his outside jacket pocket, and handed him a black, pebble-grained, zippered bag, which, when swung briskly at his side, cleared room. At the station before the ICU, a woman in white dress, white shoes, and white stockings raised one finger. "Excuse me, sir."

"Emergency consultation!" Princeton Gutkin dismissed her with a wave. A neurosurgeon at his athletic club had once confided his secret for establishing proper staff relationships. His first week granted privileges at any hospital, he kicked at least one nurse. "The only way to handle them. The know-it-all chippies. One twelve-D, well-placed."

Room 1326 was at the end of the hall. Princeton Gutkin stopped beside the window. Mt. Bilbo was in a neighborhood about one-third gentrified. Real estate speculators had evicted the welfare families from the dry-rotted Victorians, slapped on some non-union paint and trim, and sold them to commodities brokers and mortgage bankers starved for city housing. The transactions had enriched the speculators. And they had not done badly for the indigenous, self-employed entrepreneurs-in-training, lurking around Mt. Bilbo, ready to carry off the Sony, the Cuisinart, or any pocket change of the gentry the speculators might have missed.

A scrim of fog had cut other worlds from view. A stream of smoke plumed skyward. A dog — a mix of airedale, wolfhound, and Crypt Keeper — loped into a bus kiosk and howled. Be compassionate, Princeton Gutkin thought. Be knowledgeable. Listen to what the sonofabitch says. You have to sign him up. The rest of it don't mean a thing. He wondered if he would see his Porsche's engine block again.

A green curtain, three-quarters drawn, separated the two beds. On one, a shapeless lump flopped spasmodically. Stanley Doone had the second. Both his arms and legs were casted. Steel rods fixed them in place as if he had been pinned upon a mounting board. A bank of wall monitors blinked red and green, recording another die's cast. A plastic tube conveyed the gift of life, machine to man. Stanley Doone's head was taped, except for his eyes, which were open, bright and fierce.

"Good evening, Mr. Doone."

The eyes did not say anything.

"I understand you have questions about your rights." Princeton Gutkin locked the door. "There is no charge for an initial consultation."

He was unsure if the eyes nodded.

"It is important to our democratic system that every citizen keeps fully informed." Princeton Gutkin drew the curtain. "Especially going up against an outfit unscrupulous as Keep-On Trucking. I don't mean to alarm you by my attempts at security. But when serious money is riding on a case, I could tell you stories about human behavior you would not believe. You follow me, Stanley? May I? Stan? Whatever you prefer."

He was certain he saw an appreciative glint. The schlub did not seem to have a friend in the world. Either that or the orderlies on his wing were three-quarters jackal. There was not one bouquet or box of chocolates or get-well card. Not a stray petal indicated any person cared about Stanley Doone. A fatigue jacket and camouflage cargo pants, torn at both knees, were slung over a chair. A pair of red canvas sneakers, their laces knotted in a half-dozen places, sat on the floor. In the pocket of the fatigue jacket were two Rapidograph pens. Beside the bed, on a wheel-up table, were a Bible, water glass, wire-rimmed dark glasses with lenses shaped like teaspoons and thick as thumbs, and a spiral notebook open to a sketch of a big-footed, bug-eyed man pursued by snakes. Princeton Gutkin made a mental note to have Panda send a dozen roses the day following the one on which the contract was signed.

"I took the liberty of bringing some reading material for when you feel up to it." Princeton Gutkin took a brochure from his bag:

FIGHTER FOR RIGHTS
No Cause Too Small. No Foe Too Large.
THE PRINCETON GUTKIN STORY.

On the front cover, a scale of justice tipped in favor of the arm on which a silhouette of Gutkin rested. On the back, laid out like the Commandments' tablets, were"Ten DO's and DON'T's for Injury Victims." The first "'DO" was "HIRE AN EXPERIENCED ATTORNEY."

"Let me put this down, while I write a personal inscription. Say ..." Princeton Gutkin picked up the Bible. "Do you mind? It's so rare in this day and age to find someone who doesn't neglect their spiritual side. Personally, I find it crucial to centering my being. As soon as you're well, you'll have to come over and meet my ... uh, fiancee. In theological matters, Tisa's the bomb."

He opened to the black ribbon. He read in his most resonant tone. "'And the Lord continued, "'I have marked well the plight of My people ... I am mindful of their sufferings. I have come down to rescue them ... and to bring them ... to a good and spacious land, a land flowing with milk and honey...'"

Thanks a lot, God, Princeton Gutkin thought. That fat and sugar sure offered a deal. All their faith cost your chosen people were their hearts and arteries. "In all modesty, I believe we can do that for each other. Provide milk and honey, I mean. I know I feel that way about the counsel I give those looking to me."

Usually Princeton Gutkin read a prospective client's face to decide when to make his move. He would let the client take the bait, play some line, play some more, then at the proper moment, plant his feet and strike him. Stanley Doone's tape offered no clues. "But, sometimes, talk is not enough. Sometimes, action is required. We could yack all night. I could answer your questions. You'd have two dozen more. Trust me. I know how it works. The other side is building up its case, while you're lying on your back, not knowing what is happening."

The lump on the other side of the curtain moaned. Princeton Gutkin did not interrupt his presentation. Long ago, he had decided not to be easily distracted.

Every Sunday, when he was a kid, his old man, Beppo, took him to visit his father. Grandpoppy Ash, a chicken-necked, paper-chested, emphysemic ex-lumper, lived behind his grocery. The one-room store was stocked with spoiling tomatoes, blackening bananas, and oranges that reduced to pulp if too energetically squeezed. Squadrons of flies taxied from joy-spot to joy-spot. A lethargic carp, awaiting ritual execution, struggled to remain afloat in the mossy, unchanged water of a plugged-off sink.

The apartment beyond held a scratchy sofa and two flabby armchairs, all afflicted with an identical upholstery-blotching disease, and a dining table with a solitaire, four-handed pinochle game perennially in progress. The apartment was under-lit and over-heated and reeked of boiled cabbage and Cousin Farfel the Egg Man's homemade red wine. It spoke so clearly of obligation and denial that Princeton could not wait to scamper to rejoin the fish and flies and rotting vegetation at the first, "Okay, *kinder,* play."

Ash, the first Gutkin in California, had never made it off his block; but he had driven his kids to. Except for Beppo, most went pretty far. Uncle Shep to San Rafael. Uncle Duddy, Los Altos. Aunt Trixie, the Oakland hills. They had redwood trees in their backyards, Cadillacs and Lincolns in their drives, and memberships in country clubs. Enough, Princeton had realized, to keep them from dragging their kids back to Ash's every Sunday.

Beppo was a sales clerk at Woolworth's flagship, Market and Powell. He had bad breath, yellow teeth, a weasel's posture. He spent his days running through a maze of home permanent displays, pressure cooker demonstrations, and bins of candy corn, in a futile effort to satisfy his customers' longings. Publicly, he insisted his plight was temporary. He had only to catch the appropriate superior's eye. To speed discovery, half his paychecks went for grip-strengtheners and shoe-lifts, vocabulary-enrichers and dynamic mind-control techniques, each investment guaranteed to vault its possessor into executive chambers.

But Beppo remained at floor level, his income no higher, his prospects no brighter, the odds against his transformation lengthening as each Friday passed. So, privately, each Sunday, he whined how he should have gone into scrap metal like Duddy, bought a piece of Trixie's Harry's nursing homes, taken Shep up on the car wash position. Ash listened, nodded, called him his joy, his pride, his only grateful child. Beppo huddled in the wheezing old man's skeletal embrace, glowed at each feeble pat upon his spine, lapped up the oily bills pressed into his palm at the conclusion of each session.

And Princeton, one room beyond, prodding the doomed carp with a mop handle, flailing at the flies that buzzed about him in constant, disdainful waves, as if he was another clot of produce going bad, hearing the imprecations and exhortings of his adjoining elders, plotted how he would outshine every lousy cousin who had the jump on him. Swore that nothing would leave him crippled, drowning, clutching wreckage like his dad.

"So, sometime's, it's shit or get off the pot, y'hear what I'm saying? While you're making up your mind, witnesses are disappearing; evidence is being destroyed; insurance companies are going belly-up and folding." Princeton Gutkin dangled four sheets of typed, single-spaced paper, stapled together in the upper left hand corner, before Stanley Doone. The four pages contained twenty-four clauses, twenty-eight sub-clauses, and as many "hereinabove"s as a Maine field rocks. "A mere formality. The usual terms. I'd leave it and come back tomorrow, but why make a second trip? As far as I'm concerned, between gentlemen, our word could be our bond. Unfortunately, some of my brethren are not so honorably inclined. So the Bar Association in its infinite wisdom requires ..."

Princeton Gutkin attempted to place a pen in the finger nubs that protruded from the cast on Stanley Doone's right arm. He was prepared to try Elmer's Glue or hammer and nails when it caught. "You needn't date it. Initials are fine. Just hold the pen steady, and I'll move the contract until ... Ah ... Perfect!"

Strnnn Dllne.

It was hard for Princeton Gutkin to believe that simple smudge of ink had simultaneously braked his downward slide, emplated his future in twenty-four carats, removed his bank account from the Endangered Species List. He hesitated putting the contract away, as if removing it from sight would snuff its darkness-chasing flame. Things had gone too smoothly. His needs seemed too vast to be satisfied by this brief transaction. A major mockery seemed, somehow, to be building. The moan echoed from the second bed, no different than the prior, neither loud nor frantic, steady, cold, easing through the room like wind.

On the north wall, a painting of violets hung. At the bottom, in black, ran the signature: JUNE. Gutkin wondered if June had leukemia or M.S. or encephalitis. With which blossom had she been gifted exactly? He wondered how many actual bouquets had filled her room and if she expected them to flourish in her next world. He wondered if June's selection of flowers as the subject for her art indicated an abundance had caused this choice to dominate her mind, as their donors must have hoped, or if there was an irony within the child, which made her titter silently while her brushes stroked.

"You won't regret your choice. We will make the guilty pay." As he spoke, Gutkin replaced "roses" in his mental note for Panda with "daisies." In the bracket to which he was about to be restored, a dollar saved was many earned. "Don't forget. Soon as you're out, call me. We'll do lunch."

VODK
EEP
MAN IS
BA-A-A-D
SERVE NOTE
100
100
10
'16
RL
CRABB

Chapter V.

"The good news is we're prepared to collapse the policy for your poor fellow." Tickerton C. Myrth, III, had an artificial arm. When he represented plaintiffs in front of juries, it dropped everything he touched. When he worked the other side of the street — when, for instance, he was on a thirty-five hundred *per diem* for Fountain of Youth Casualty — he could use it to do needlepoint or smash cinder blocks. "The bad news is the limits are a hundred thousand."

"One hundred-K." Princeton Gutkin hit his vodka martini. Tic Myrth was drinking malt whiskey, neat. Chickie Gilligan had an Anchor Steam. They were in the back of the Club Moulin on Upper Fillmore. It was two nights after Gutkin's visit to Mt. Bilbo. A quartet was playing something Latin for the few couples on the floor. The pianist seemed not to know the drummer, the saxophonist never introduced to either, and the bassist burned in a meth deal by all three. The couples lurched about as if avoiding blows. "The hospital bill alone tops that."

"On behalf of everyone at Fountain of Youth, I extend heartfelt condolences. But no matter how hard any jury hits us, that is all we'll have to pay." Tic Myrth wore ox-blood loafers, pink and green argyle socks, canary yellow slacks, a green shirt, pink knit tie, and navy blazer. He had graying blonde hair and a puffy face, so red from St. Francis Yacht Club sun his color might have been created by Perry Ellis. When he opened his hands, like in the commercial, there was nothing there. Not in the one with five fingers. Not in the one with steel claws. "So to save my client paperwork and fees, I have a draft in my pocket, which, in point of fact, we were prepared to deliver to Mr. Injured Party before you even called."

"They shouldn't let a trucking company loose to maim innocent civilians with lousy coverage like that," Princeton Gutkin said.

"In point of fact, their best maiming days may be behind them. They've already filed Chapter 11." "Scratch seizing their assets," Chickie Gilligan said.

"A hundred-fucking-K." Princeton Gutkin looked at the posters on the wall, Guatamalan rivers, mountains in Nepal, a beach at Cannes. He felt like Tic Myrth's news had fade-dissolved them into refineries in Trenton, waste treatment plants in Fall River, Calcutta's alluring Black Hole. He closed his eyes. The mockery, which he had sensed hovering in Stanley Doone's hospital room, now rested with one hand comraderally on his shoulder, while the other lifted his billfold from his back pocket. What he would clear, once the client got his share and Chickie his cut, would not last long with Tisa. To have come so close and fallen so short was more tortuous than if his opportunity had never arisen. Gutkin was convinced he would never see another case as good. He felt unfairly trapped and toyed with: a mouse being cuffed by a great cat-God, awaiting the final, spine-severing blow

"I was over at the Hall," Chickie Gilligan was saying. "Judge Rubino had this fag, S&M murder case in Department 14. Whips, chains, bottles in orifices unexplored by the common man. He's addressing the jury and he goes, 'Ladies and gentlemen, I apologize for the nature of the testimony you've heard. Maybe, next time, we'll have a simple rear-ender for you. And the whole place cracks up."

"Picture this poor kid, Tickler, a minute. He had his whole life in front of him: a career and family." "Princeton, old *caballero*, his job could give him ulcers, his wife split with the tennis pro, his kids shoot up with Valvoline. Your poor fellow should be thankful we aren't claiming a credit for all the heartaches that our driver saved him." "He was just crossing the street," Princeton Gutkin said. "In the crosswalk. On the green. The sun was shining. The sky was blue. He was whistling 'Happy Days.' And your scumbag creams him." "We at the Fountain commend you for your compelling presentation. The logic and the poetry. We, also, could not care less if he was delivering Girl Scout cookies to the leper colony. So let's cut the hearts-and-flowers. In point of fact, it's all piss in the wind." "A hundred-K. A hundred-K. How'm I gonna break the news to the kid? How can I look him in the eye?" "You can't look him much of any place else," Chickie Gilligan said.

"How can I say to him ... uh ... uh ..."

"'Stanley ...'"

"'Stanley ... all you get is a fucking hundred-K.'"

"Less, of course, your fee and costs," Tic Myrth said.

"Damn right, my fee and costs. I put a lot into this case. I brought it home with me. These are the ones that haunt you." "I can imagine," Tic Myrth said.

"Damn right, you can imagine. Me and this kid are close. I feel so bad that wreck might as well have crippled me. How can I tell him he won't clear sixty thou?"

"'You clear over fifty thou,'" Chickie Gilligan said. "'Sign here.'" "It's a fucking crime. That's what it is, you know that."

"Anyone for another round? Princeton? Francis Xavier?"

"I may sue anyway. Fight to the Supreme Court. Make new law. Establish my reputation for posterity. A fitting way to cap my career."

"Can I see you in my office?" Chickie Gilligan said.

"Are you crazy? Grab the fucking dough."

The Men's Room's stall had no door. The mirror had been smashed by a fist or Dos Equis bottle. The window did not shut and the waste basket overflowed with paper towels. A genius had screwed a blackboard above the urinal without taking into account that any population with a number of wall-writers would have its share of chalk-stealers too. So all the writing was where the genius hoped to keep it from:

GOD MADE SHEEP
CAUSE WOMAN IS B-A-A-A-D

THIS IS THE WORST PLACE I EVER ATE.
DO YOU OFTEN EAT IN TOILETS, DUDE?

EARTH: SHOULD HAVE CLOSED IN NEW HAVEN

"Chickie, listen, there is right and wrong. There is such a thing as injustice." "Police! Help! This man's been possessed by Mahatma Ghandi!" Chickie Gilligan turned the cold water tap. When the rust had cleared, he dipped in a wad of toilet paper. "Put this some place'll start you thinking clear." "One hundred-lousy-K." Princeton Gutkin dabbed at his forehead.

"Stop saying that. Take the man's check. With your share and two aspirin, you'll feel better in the morning." Princeton Gutkin stopped wiping. He made a feeble grab with his other hand.

"That's the boy. Look at the bright side. Tomorrow is another day. Candlestick Park could get taken out by a chemical explosion in South City. Alameda County get zapped by a nuclear meltdown at Livermore. It's a great age to be a P.I. attorney. I wish I was a young fellow like you, starting fresh with all the advantages modern technology can bestow."

"There is nothing wrong with a hundred thousand dollars." "Now you're talking. Remember that old legal maxim. 'It's better than a stick in the eye.' Of course, that sounds one hell of a lot classier in Latin." "I don't know what got into me. I'm fine. Give me two seconds to pull it together." "Take seven. I'll swap war stories with the loyal opposition. Let him tell me how that judge in Stockton cold-cocked him with the Evidence Code."

The shattered mirror split Princeton Gutkin's reflection into disjointed shards. He tired to remember where everything was. The vodka and the disappointment had blurred his thinking. But he was thinking cleanly now. There were his nose, both eyes, his ears. He felt himself restore Vermeer's order to a Cubist world. He plumped his pompadour with his two hands.

He had come too far to let it end here. It had taken him six years to get his B.A. And four more for his L.L.B. — bussing tables, hawking class rings, peddling tuna salad subs in dorms. And when he got out, he only landed work because his Uncle Shep pulled strings with this *schlock* firm in the avenues that handled his car washes. The firm gave him a desk next to the Xerox and a three hundred dollar a month draw against half what he cleared on its overflow. Collections, child support, and fender-benders.

D.U.I.s, personal bankruptcies, and no-witness slip-and-falls. The first one of those he tried, the deputy city attorney got his client on cross and went, "Now, Mrs. Davenport, isn't it true you filed another claim against the City in April for a fall on Polk Street?" "That's right, sonny. And they wouldn't pay me a red cent." "And in May for a fall on Van Ness?" "You bet. And I didn't collect a nickel." "And in June, you reported *three* falls in United Nations Plaza?" By the time the deputy let Mrs. Davenport leave, Judge Brogan bellowed, "Counsel, aren't you going to help your client down?" Like he was afraid she was going to trip and bust her heinie and sue them all. He was out with the flu four weeks his first year and nobody at the firm knew he was gone.

But he had hung in there. Toughed it out. Turned it around. Not without a little luck. Not without, what-you-call, the Sixties happening. He had not believed it when he saw what was going on. Before, in law school, the whole idea was you finished highest in your class, you joined the biggest firm, you raked in the biggest pile. All of a sudden, all the bright, young lawyers were lining up behind PEACE and LOVE. TENANT'S UNIONS and PRISONERS' RIGHTS. WAR PROTESTS and DRAFT RESISTING. He liked the idea of the bright, young lawyers devoting themselves to noble causes. It left more room for someone to do business in the accustomed manner.

He opened up a storefront in the Haight. He let his hair grow and stopped wearing ties and hung posters of doves on the walls. He signed petitions and attended protests and did his laps on picket lines. The bright, young lawyers did not want to drain their energies for THE MOVEMENT into anything grubby as auto accidents. They did not mind referring cases to a righteous cat like him.

For five, ten years, everything was copacetic. Then — WHAM — there was no draft to resist and no war to protest. Prisoners were shooting their lawyers, and the thrill of stalling some indigent's eviction faded further with each three new notices-to-quit sitting in your waiting room. Fewer attorneys were interested in creating a new society, and more were acquiring 250SLs and time-share ski chalets and enrolling their kids in pre-schools that would track them toward a Stanford M.B.A. They fought like ferrets for the claims they hoped to mine.

At first, he had withstood the competition. He had positioned in the market early. He had his reputation and name. But the number of lawyers kept rising. Their ads stuffed the Yellow Pages. Their faces shot up on billboards and bus sides and the back ends of cabs. He was out of the low-overhead Haight now and into cushy Jackson Square. And it was a fact of life that the number of catastrophes occurring in any given stretch of time could not satisfy all the attorneys who hoped to live off them. He felt like one of a small band of Cherokees, following a herd of buffalo across the plain for generations. Then here came a thousand Comanches with whom he had to share.

He had quickly seen the trick was squeezing more juice out of his slice of the filet. Either that or start thinking Chicken of the Sea again. So he had developed techniques which, while successful in maintaining his standard of living, were unlikely to be honored at a skills seminar of the Practicing Law Institute. So he swore to claims adjustors that a client would not settle for less than ten thousand dollars — even if the client had not dreamed of over three. So he cut any offer in half before conveying it to the client, thereby assuring himself gratitude, respect and future business by unfailingly winning more. So he, eventually, asked himself why this client, who would welcome three thousand dollars should reap the windfall of the ten produced by his savvy and negotiating skills? Let the client believe the settlement was for seventy-five hundred or six thousand or thirty-two fifty, depending on his and Tisa's current shopping list. And by substituting doctored releases and forging signatures on settlement drafts the insurance companies sent, that was what he did. The first time he pocketed the extra bread he expected the S.F.P.D. to kick in the door. When they didn't, hey, the second time was easy.

The moral was simple: LIFE WAS GROWTH. You caught onto that, you made yourself a better situation. Otherwise, you might as well have never left your crib. The way he saw it, all people lived in prisons of which they were unaware. They were locked inside believing certain patterns of behavior were the only way to be. Sometimes — like him with his settlements — you recognized one of these confining walls and burst through. You thought, until you hit the next wall, you were free. You had to keep chipping at walls, and that could get scary. Because you never knew what could be behind the next one.

There was a fly speck on the glass. Princeton Gutkin realized he had overlooked possibilities in the Stanley Doone scenario. The guy would be in Mt. Bilbo six months. Six months was a long time. Many investment opportunities were available to someone with one hundred thousand dollars at his disposal for six months. When the six months had passed and it became necessary to disburse the settlement, Stanley Doone could have his share; and he could have his, plus the profits from the investing.

Then there was the possibility that Stanley Doone would not leave the hospital. He did not like to think about it. But facts were facts. The man's injuries were severe. The course of recovery did not always run smooth. He had to consider, too, that Stanley Doone had no heirs. That no outsiders even knew he had signed the contract.

Princeton Gutkin pursed his lips to check the whiteness of his teeth.

PART

TWO.

Six months later ...

EL DIA DE

Chapter VI.

A hexagon, in whose center was an eye, filled the front window of the shop. The wind blew the rain against the window, hard. Like bullets in the eye, thought the man in the knit skull cap, layered red and green, blue and orange, black and gold. If I enter the shop now, I will be a bullet.

In the eye.

Jars of chalky glass lined the shop's shelves. Smoked mice and embalmed tarantulas and pickled crows filled the jars. Kitten teeth and badger mandibles and owl claws. Bat ovaries and eagle hearts and iguana scrotum. Anything anyone had ever imagined chewing or licking, sucking or sipping. Whole or dried. Powdered or encapsulated. Anything anyone had believed brought love or increased wealth or conveyed power or restored health or wreaked evil or fashioned good.

The light was dim within the shop and the air cloudy. The only sound was the hiss of candles burning. The stretched and tanned hide of a giant toad was nailed to the wall. A tiny, squat woman stood before it. She had a wide mouth and bulbous eyes. She had greenish skin, mottled by lines and liver spots. The hide might have been a cloak she had flung aside. She might have been its more mobile, juicier cousin. "You buy?" she peeped. "How much? How many? Please."

"I need time for my decision." Below his rainbow-layered skullcap, the customer wore a black suit jacket, black pipe stem pants, a white wash-and-wear shirt sprinkled with scorch marks, black-and-red Air Jordans, double laced. His face was set as rigid as a man hole cover. The words, hollow and flat, squeezed out of his mouth like eggs from a fly. "I can not afford the least mistake."

"Very nice. Feeling better. One-two-three."

"I have this serious condition." He had to be certain She had sent the rain to bring him into the store. His mother-She. Not the toad woman-She. The rain had come from the sky. His mother lived in the sky. She had told him She would send the sign when it was time for his next erasure. To resume his sacred and professional duties. She had warned him they would use power and trickery to stop him. If this toad could turn into a woman, it had strength and skill and cunning.

"Hey, pal, take alla time you need." A young man had sprung up from behind the counter. He had greenish skin. He was tall and weedy with fidgety hands. He wore Ray Ban sunglasses whose convex, mirrored lenses cupped his eyes like a mantis'. Clipped to the mantis' breast pocket was a white plastic case that said "Upjohn." In the case were four pens, a thermometer, tweezers, calipers. The customer assumed the transmitter was in one of the pens. "At Li and Fils, the product sells itself or we don't stock it."

"I need to take my time."

"We recognize your old fashioned, mom-and-pop ju-ju store is not about to happen in your dot com. Age. So we are setting standards for the entire industry. I am talking demographics and market research, web sites and computerized warehousings. I am talking Biff and Muffy Whitebread in Los Altos, Stu and Suzie Bland in Orinda. I see our product in their lives as much as Banana Republic and Beemers. What, you think they don't have our problems in the 'burbs?"

"I appreciate your concern."

"Pal, I think we understand each other. I think we can talk. Mama-san, here, keeps the old line customers happy, but I see you as strictly po-mo. You have any questions, you come to me. The first rule at Li and Fils is: 'Walk Out Happy.' Because rule number two is: 'We Want You Racing Back.'"

"That is more than fair." The customer glanced at the window. The rain rattled without effect. The eyeball did not bleed. He had passed the store many times in the past six months. His mother had warned they meant to lure him in. His mother had assured she would announce the time for his sacred and professional entry. His mother had long brown hair, which she wound around him when they danced each evening, alone, in their cabin on the grounds of the Community. At the Community, all the Gladiettes were brides of Father Dynamite. All Gladiators were his right arms. All the Pups his seeds. All Gladiators and Gladiettes and Pups were brothers and sisters and cousins who labored for his glory. Across the street, a man clutching a fatigue jacket to his throat raced for the shelter of a doorway. He caught the toe of his red sneaker on the corner of a grate and went sprawling. The fall almost appeared natural and honest. Like the fool's mission was not to maintain surveillance and file his report.

"If you will answer a few questions, I will suggest a program custom-tailored to your individual needs." The mantis set a sheet of paper, folded over and over upon itself, on the counter. "Age?"

The customer hesitated.

"The information is strictly confidential and available only to members of our staff." *It is all right*, his mother said.

"Twenty-four."

"Height?"

"Six-two."

"Six-feet, two-inches. Very good. Weight?"

"Two hundred-twenty pounds."

"Just a growing boy. Do you or any member of your family suffer from mood swings? Irritable bowels? Night sweats ..." *You can tell the fool*, his mother said. *Just because the fools speak no truth, does not mean you should not answer.*

"All the time ..." The customer had close cropped black hair. His eyes were the color of sludge. His nose was scarred as if someone had tried to bite it off. "... my nipples sting. My heart whistles tunes I wish forgotten."

"Pal, it sounds like you've got yourself a problem and a half." The mantis held up a dark vial between his thumb and index finger. "Have you considered desiccated yak phlegm?"

Jerome Heavens shook his head. He had considered nothing. He had entered the store because he had been on the street and his mother had announced it time for the erasure. He spent all his time on the street now. His pain was too bad to work. His pain was too bad to sleep. It had been seven months since that doctor operated. It had been six months since that lawyer turned his case down. He had stopped going to lawyers and doctors. None of those fools could help him. Like Father Dynamite taught, they were all chasing the damn dollar. All abandoning their sacred and professional duty. Not one helping the injured man. It had been nine months since he had been hurt and the job sent him to the doctor and the doctor hurt him more. Since leaving the Community, Kwilty-Humberg had been his life. Every pallet, raised or lowered, fed him. With each shipment, in or out, he breathed. He obeyed his foreman's directives absolutely. He followed his leadman's every word. He cared little for anyone else. He ate his lunches alone; he exchanged no nods; he met no glances. Every morning's alarm sent him from his China Basin room to the company. Every evening's whistle returned him to China Basin. He had been six years at Kwilty-Humberg, and it threw him away like he was a rag or dog or torn and dirty doll. He was lying in the hospital, remembering Father Dynamite's teachings, when his mother had returned.

He would like to put a bullet in the eye of every damn one.

"Seventy-five an ounce. It's on special this week. Two for $125. We were able to buy in bulk because of the strong showing of the dollar."

"That sounds like a lot of money."

"Not when you consider the advantages. This baby will stimulate your organs. Your spleen. Your pancreas. Pal, I don't have to tell you what else. And our products come fully warranted. Money back in sixty days if not completely satisfied. But you should stock up now. Once OPEC gets its act together, they will jack the price up through the roof."

"It still sounds like a lot. For I don't know what."

"Yak," the toad woman said. "Shaggy. Big animal. Like cow." She indicated horns, sweeping toward the ceiling, from each side of her head.

Jerome Heavens wondered if she intended to turn into a cow. He wondered if she would let him see her turn into the Devil, horned.

"Best thing in the world for nipples," the mantis said. "You know who endorses our line? Shirley MacLaine. I wouldn't sell it if Shirley didn't stamp it with her personal okie-dokie. She never goes any place without a kilo. Rubs it on her nips before she steps on stage. Pal, you know I couldn't say it if it wasn't true. The F.T.C. come down on me like crazy."

"I just need this time to consider." Father Dynamite taught the problems of the world were caused by men not fair to other men. Who charged them too much for too little. Who hurt them and did not make them well. Who used up people and threw them away. Father Dynamite had lived with his mother for three years. She had been his Bride Among Brides. She had been her happiest. She cooked for Father Dynamite and washed for him and scrubbed his toilet bowl. She performed her sacred and professional duties. It was here the next erasures would begin.

"I understand exactly. Believe me, I'm the last guy in the world to rush a pal. But time is money too, right? Listen, you want something a little more low rent, we could put you in wasp mucous. A trifle *declasse* but it will do the job. Very popular with our older customers. People on fixed incomes. Set you back $49.95"

The young man, whose name was C. Richelieu Li, loved to sell. He had a Wharton M.B.A. and had logged time at U. Chicago. Milton Friedman was his man. He loved the challenge. He loved the creativity. He loved vibing out what got the mark to unbutton his pocket. He knew he was *this* close. He also knew you could not tell what goodies were inside the pocket by reading the coat. In his business, you threw out that they looked weird. You threw out that they talked weird or smelled weird. In his business, weird was the whole thing. Just last Thursday, he had unloaded a six pack of blowfish bouillabaisse on a chucklehead walked in wearing orange flip-flops, so shaky he looked like, for a living, he could handle, maybe, hooking pop cans out of sewers on sticks. The guy paid him with two fifties off a roll as thick as Johnny Wadd's best feature. Miltie the Mortician, here, C. Richelieu Li thought, could be packing enough Krugeraands to land you on the moon.

"I know what you're thinking. Still high, am I right? But you think collecting wasp mucous is easy? You ever see one of the little buggers sneeze? Just a little joke. A little levity. Listen, you pay cash, no plastic, I'll let it go for $40, give you a receipt for the full price, and throw in a 'script from a genuine physician that'll let you write off the whole transaction with Uncle as a medical deduction. Did I tell you, pal, that's one outrageous lid you're wearing?"

Jerome Heavens looked at his reflection in the Ray Ban lenses. He had not been in a voodoo shop in a long time. His mother had taken him to one in Fort Callie when he was sixteen. Many men had left him and his mother after Father Dynamite said it was Her time to be shared. The last Gladiator to share her, Brother Cleve, played a silver flute, wore a necklace made from pigeon bones, had a black and gold mandala embroidered on his leather vest, kept a snub-nosed Walther in the saddle bags of his Harley-Davidson. Cleve left, his mother said, because Sister Helene placed a running curse on him. "She sprinkled his boots, his pants, his saddle bags, Jerome, so he ran from us. Every time I see Cleve now, he starts running."

What his mother bought in the voodoo store did not bring back Cleve. She grew sick instead. She said Sister Helene had paid the voodoo man in Fort Callie to put Vanishing Dust on her. Jerome Heavens watched his mother lie on her bed and shrivel. He heard the cough, night-after-night, rasp out her bones. He smelled the fever, day-after-day, burn away her flesh. He sat beside her while the brothers and sisters in the Community paid the single visit Father Dynamite allowed. He watched them kiss his mother's forehead and set down their gifts for her journey: the candle; the slippers; the penny. He watched them close her behind the door. He heard Father Dynamite say nothing could be done. When he told Father Dynamite about the voodoo man, Father Dynamite locked him in the tool shed. For three days, there was no light. For three days, there was no play. For three days, there was only Father Dynamite bringing him a cup of tepid water, a slice of mold-greened bread, a shaft of string-meated bone. Once he awoke from a shivering sleep, and his mother floated before him. "Erase," she told him. "Purify. Do your sacred and professional duty."

The day he was released from the shed, his mother died. His mother, who pressed him to her breast and wrapped him in her hair and danced him around the cabin's floor until he was so drunk from Her smells he could not see or think. His mother, who took him to the hills, lay down with him at the top, rolled beside him to the bottom, and laughed crazily with him as they tried to stand and fell, tried to stand and fell, then stood and raced back up. On her last night of this life, his mother had called his name, lain her arms around his shoulders, drawn his head toward hers, and, at the moment he expected her kiss, sank her teeth into his face and howled.

Two days after the death of his mother, Jerome Heavens lifted Brother Cleve's Walther from the saddle bag on his Harley Davidson, drove the Comet the four miles into Fort Callie, and shot the voodoo man in the right eye. Then, after firing the apple orchard, he left the Community.

"Listen, pal, this is one popular item. You can't count on us having stock tomorrow. You know who buys this? The Diocese. Of course, they shop by the back door. Your clergy doesn't want Joe Public knowing the good stuff it's into. It deflates the mystery. But it keeps running off the shelves, I kid you not. People are recognizing the values of traditional remedies."

He knew the mantis was lying. They were all lying. They did not help the injured man. The doctors. The lawyers. The merchants polluting the temples. They did not care about his mother. They did not care about his pain. They used you up and threw you away. He had not thought before. He was thinking now. The mantis believed he was a fool.

Jerome Heavens howled and shot the mantis through the right lens of his Ray-Bans.

The toad tried to hide. She had turned into a woman. She had almost turned into a Devil. She tried to crawl under the table.

He blew out the back of her head.

Coca-Cola
TED RICHARDS © 2016

Chapter VII.

Stanley Doone ripped the wrapper from another chocolate doubloon. His fatigue jacket and camouflage pants were soaked. His hip ached at the point where he had landed when he tripped over the grate. Both his hips had already ached — and both arms, both legs, his back and neck — from where the truck had hit him. But the recognition of new pain pleased him. The realization he could be in constant pain and still hurt more confirmed his belief that existence was an agony you bore unconsciously, like the weight of air, until it fucking broke you. He dropped the foil into the ash tray, where a half-dozen crumpled gold balls already lay.

"Mr. Gutkin says it could be a while."

"I'll wait."

"He said to tell you there's no news on your case."

"I waited yesterday, man. I waited the day before. I'll wait." Absorbed by the mirror behind the bar, Panda glued on a false eyelash as if he was not there. "And, oh yeah, he said, 'Tell him there's a letter in the mail.'"

"Tell your boss I'm still waiting on the letter he fucking promised me Tuesday. In case he wants to take it up with the postal authorities." On the knuckles of Stanley Doone's right hand had been tatooed H-A-T-E. On the knuckles of his left hand was the same. He had a half-inch wide strip of dyed-orange stubble in the middle of his chin. His inky black hair had been plastered flat by the rain. His gray-white skin had been stretched tight by his months in Mt. Bilbo. His confinement had stitched more resignation into his face than rejuvenation, injected more fatigue into his veins than spirit, debrided less desperation from his cuts than ease. One half of his dark glasses bent forward so that entire socket seemed to jump across the room. "While you're at it, man, you might mention I'd appreciate him squeezing me in this afternoon. See, tomorrow I can't make it. I have this appointment." He adjusted his glasses to draw Panda closer. "With the Bar Association."

When Stanley Doone was ten-years-old, the rest of the fourth grade had drowned in the greatest tragedy in Moltoc County history. They had gone to the beach near Clam Junction for the year end picnic. They had been warned not to turn their backs on the ocean. No one knew if Mr. Pittlings, while arranging the class portrait, did not scream loud enough or soon enough or was too busy placing "Short-people-up-front. Tall-people-behind" to see the rising wave.

Stanley Doone had been sick at home. He did not receive the news until breakfast the next morning. He did not cry. He knew he was supposed to, but nothing made it happen. His father, who spliced cables with Rural Electrification, and his mother, a Clerk-Typist II with the D.M.V., complimented him for being such a brave little fellow. They told each other he was old enough to deal with things his own way. That it showed good judgment not to dwell on gloom. They took down his school pennant, transferred him to a district where he would face fewer unpleasant reminders, and did not discuss the subject in his presence again.

For the next few weeks, Stanley Doone went about his business cautiously. Moltoc City was full of visiting reporters and black-draped windows and memorial services. His lack of emotion worried him. Part of him feared he had been only temporarily spared and was due a personal, more painful punishing. Part expected to be flooded by tears at any moment. Once he stubbed a toe, wept more than normally, and wondered if his account was squared. But the headlines shifted, the crepe came down, and he knew he would have no greater response. When he thought about his classmates, he saw no good reason why he should. His core memories were the boys plunking him at dodgeball, the girls giggling when he walked by, and all of them, the boys and girls, ridiculing the comic books he poured over at lunch or recess and, pointing at his thick glasses, skinny body, hissing "Doone-the-Goon."

He was no longer ashamed or puzzled. He felt he had achieved a valuable insight. His own vision could be more compelling than that of any compliant herd's. When the reporters came to record the drowning's fifth anniversary, Stanley Doone told them, "I don't think about it. I've got other things on my mind." "Like what?" one reporter asked. "Like my illustrations of the alimentary canal for the Arts Fair." When they came back for the tenth, he had left Moltoc County; and with both his parents passed, no one knew where he could be found.

Which was not to say that Stanley Doone regarded the drownings as trivial. These were children he knew, after all, not kittens in a sack. He was certain he did not fully understand the impact of the drownings on himself; but, as he grew older, he would reflect that this must have been the most important event of his formative years. The failure of as formidable a home room teacher as Mr. Pittlings to avoid the occurrence accounting for his scorn for authorities. His being singled out for survival demonstrating that his life was to be unique and consequential. The entire experience crucial to the minting of his calling — the creation of his projected four-volume, all-cartoon treatise: *Lunacies, Failures and Disasters*: *Encounters With the Modern Age.*

"You've heard about court backlog?" Princeton Gutkin said. "*60 Minutes* called it 'a national disgrace.' This county is so jammed that, if we said your case was ready for trial — and it's not — not quite-quite ready; and I filed our At-Issue Memorandum, demanding the first available courtroom, you wouldn't see a jury for three years."

"Fuck the courts, man." Stanley Doone slammed his fist on the captain's desk. "To hell with *60 Minutes.* I want my money." "I understand your frustration." Princeton Gutkin nipped the tip from a Monte Christo. He lay an even layer of saliva around its outer leaf, lit a match to the blunt end, and watched it crinkle red. "But I don't want you making rash decisions. Cutting off your nose to spite your face would personally hurt me." Stanley Doone did not reply. He was visualizing *Lunacies and Failures.* Sheets of paper, penciling in progress, spread across his desk. Sheets of penciled paper, inked, Wite-outed and re-inked, clothes-pinned sequentially to the lengths of twine that criss-crossed his apartment. Sheets of paper, reviewed, revised, re-reviewed, and, having passed final inspection, stacked, page-upon-page, in the portfolios propped against his walls.

Within these pages' panels, cross-hatched and shadowed, the figures of his imagination, through their halting, unedifying speech and bumbling, unavailing actions, with their bulging eyes and dripping snouts, their gaping mouths and flapping ears, in every line of their sagging, slouching, born-to-be-defeated bearings, traversed the narrative line of each of their individual stories towards the uniformly stomach-sinking, brain-numbing conclusions which dramatized Stanley's over-arching thesis. Death was the most important fact of life. It was, in his opinion, a position sweeping in scope, irrefutable in argument, revolutionary in conclusion. He was on page 626, which put him roughly two-thirds through the opening volume.

Two things were clear to Stanley Doone. First, man would exist only for a blink in the infinity of time. Second, the earth was not even one grain of sand in the desert of the cosmos. But despite these unsurmountable, undeniable limitations, people insisted on acting as if they meant something. They attached importance to such nonsense as "family," "country," "profession," "art." This was because they needed shields to protect them from the horror of their fucking nothingness. From the annihilation that waited. As long as they could hide behind their nonsense, they did not have to face how completely they would be gone. But their efforts were straws in the wind. Delusionary straws. It was as though an evil wizard had cast a spell over the people so they believed they would never face the truth of their condition.

But they would face it.

Every-fucking-one.

At some point, each person's straws were blown away. Everybody learned their life, which had once seemed limitless, was nothing; and all they sought to fill it with was null. The sooner they learned this, the better. The sooner they escaped the grasp of the wizard, the longer they would have to prepare to keep the moment of their learning from crushing them. The longer they would have to redirect their futile, desperate strivings toward a more gratifying world. It was up to him to finish *Lunacies and Failures* and, through its impact, alert the fucking people.

For a dozen years, he had supported his work with temporary jobs — bike messenger; usher in an all-night movie; distributor of flyers, "Free

Coke With Pizza Slice," "Admit Two: Midnight Madness" — speeding *Lunacies and Failure*'s completion. Now, the money from his law suit would let him write and draw without interruption. Stanley Doone believed that the greater forces, which had spared him from his classmates' drownings, had sent him into that intersection the same moment as that truck to confirm the importance of his mission.

Which made him angrier at these delays.

"Dude, if you care about me so fucking much, why haven't I heard from you? Why don't you return my fucking calls?" "Stanley, I'm sorry. But I do have other clients."

"You act like you're avoiding me, man."

"Avoiding you? Didn't we have lunch at Max's Opera Plaza?" "Two months ago."

"Didn't I have you over the apartment? What, three, four times? Me and you and Tisa. You think I *schmooze* like that with everyone?" Princeton Gutkin tried his warmest smile. It was like flinging a match at Bodega Bay and hoping for a conflagration. "You told us about your comic ..."

"My *graphic* quartet."

"Whatever. A rose by any other name. Fascinating. Brilliant. I'm still mulling over the thinking. I was holding off getting together until I had digested it so's I could hold up my end of the conversation."

Stanley Doone scratched his orange stubble with a bitten nail.

"What you got there. Fabulous. A concept of major proportions. I didn't want to say anything premature, but I've been speaking to an associate in Hollywood. He loves the material. Loves it. Don't say anything right away. Think it over. How does Robin Williams sound as your Alistaire Cooke-type spokesperson? Robin in a beard and robe and sandals hosting all your little stories. Maybe shop it to HBO for a series. Stanley, Stanley, Stanley, I give you all this personal attention, and this is how you act. You got to understand. Law suits take time."

"To hell with Robin Williams. Fuck HBO. I've had it with time, man." BAM! "I want action." "Believe me, you'll get it."

"I keep hearing that, man. But I need money."

"I'd offer you a few dollars, but the Bar frowns on that sort of thing. It feels it would impose a conflict of interest between us." Keeping his smile on his face felt to Princeton Gutkin like tacking a jellyfish to a wall. "Plus, if lawyers could lend money to clients, you see how it is, only rich lawyers would have them."

Princeton Gutkin blew a smoke ring at the ceiling. As soon as Stanley Doone's hand had come out of its cast, he had started writing letters. As soon as his breathing tube had been removed, he phoned. Every day. Twice a day. Three times. The tone was always petulant or accusatory or demanding. The message was always money, money, money. Since he had been released from Mt. Bilbo, Stanley had got worse. It did not matter what he tried. Giving out his cell number. Fed Ex-ing weekly status reports. Hosting him to all those turkey Reubens. Staying awake while he droned on and on about this comic book. This comic about death and all. It was so depressing it was funny. He had even got Tisa to act like she gave a flying fuck. But none of it had worked. Stanley was dropping by the office so frequently and so out of control that, each time the intercom buzzed, his desk winced. The message was always the same. Money, money, money. For someone who was supposed to be a deep thinker, the guy showed little interest in the finer things of life.

Yeah, Stanley had become a classic case of, what was called in the field, your CLIENT CONTROL PROBLEM. "I've got myself a minor Client-Control Problem," you would tell defense counsel when Mr. Baumholz refused to answer interrogatories, attend his deposition, show up for his independent medical. "Sounds like a Client-Control Problem," the settlement conference judge would announce when Mrs. Foujami would not take the thirty-five hundred for her backache, three-fifty in medicals, zero wage loss, because her cousin Ahmed had got two hundred-fifty grand for the exact same injury and was back playing nose guard for the Raiders, while she could not bend down to paint her toes. Sometimes he ignored Client-Control Problems. Occasionally he told them, "Get the hell out of my office! Find another lawyer!" Once in a while, if he had a score to settle, he personally recommended one. But for Client-Control Problems with big cases, he had learned to eat a little shit. On this one, hey, he was practically feeding himself with a shovel.

The difficulty was not his having settled Stanley Doone's case without telling Stanley. He had made a few errors of judgment besides. Like the pork-belly futures that soured like they had been soaked in brine. Like the real-estate syndicate which collapsed like it had been hit by a wrecker's ball. Like Client-Control Problem Stanley walking out of Mt. Bilbo quick enough to make *The New England Journal.*

"I demand my day in court, man." BAM! "I know my rights. I'm a fucking American citizen." "I thought we ran through that. The backlog. The delay."

"Fuck, dude, I want my money. They owe me my money. I have plans for my money, man. You hear the fuck what I am saying?"

"You would like your money." Princeton Gutkin contemplated his client through his Monte Christo's smoke. The guy was such a geek you could practically see feathers when he belched. Stanley Doone was one of those people whose personalities benefitted from a little plaster, a little tape, and being bolted down. He lacked heart; he lacked soul; and he was shrill. He was not what-you-would-consider loveable. You could dress him up, maybe mousse that hair, shave that pussy-tickler; but those cockamamie Robert Mitchum *Night of the Hunter* tats were forever. Forget it. Stanley was not the sort of person you would want to sit next to in a bus terminal, let alone put before a jury.

As if that was a possibility.

"One thing we don't want is to conclude your case before it's medically wise. Suppose you had to go back in the hospital. Suppose, God forbid, another surgery. You call up the insurance company to renegotiate, you know what they will tell you? 'Sorry, fellah. Love to help. But our hands are tied.'" Princeton Gutkin gestured, wrists together, fingers wiggling, like he had been manacled. It was not an image that he welcomed. "Besides, it takes two to tango."

"You mean the shitbags might not settle?"

"The longer they hold onto your money, the more interest they earn. The more interest they earn, you don't have to be Albert Einstein to figure, the less they've paid you at the end. I made one hell of a reasonable demand. I can't stick a gun to their heads."

"So what'd you ask them for exactly, man?"

"Two-point-five mill." Princeton Gutkin knocked ash from his cigar on one of Pritikin's metatarsals. Clients liked it when you talked in millions, and he liked to keep his clients happy. It did not cost two cents for Panda to type extra zeros on a prayer. "Until they come up with an offer, I don't budge off our figure. We don't negotiate against ourselves."

Stanley Doone nodded.

"So, you see, we agree." Princeton Gutkin liked it when his clients nodded too. He closed a drawer, straightened some papers, and hunched forward in his chair. His moves said: consensus reached; transaction concluded; time to go.

But Stanley Doone did not budge. "Dude, I am not greedy. Do not get me wrong. All I want, is my fair share, man, so I can finish *Lunacies and Failures.*"

"Ab-so-lute-ly *clear.* I don't doubt you for a moment. Even Mr. Myrth, normally a suspicious guy, thinks you're a beautiful person. And if that's it ..." Princeton Gutkin again closed and hunched and straightened. He extended a hand so there would be no further misunderstanding.

Only Stanley Doone still sat there. "So, what's our next plan of attack?"
"Discovery." Relax, Princeton Gutkin told himself. The putz still does not know what's happening. "They've sent us a third set of interrogatories. I've sent a third to them. There are several more depositions to take and experts to disclose; both sides have motions for sanctions pending with the commissioner." "But I want this over, man. I want to get on with my life."

"Hellova healthy attitude. Wish more of my clients shared it. You've got no idea how many people become overly involved in their litigation. But I'm not sure you appreciate how vigorously plead and thoroughly contested your case has become." Princeton Gutkin waved his Monte Christo at a redwood bookcase. The two top shelves were filled by accordion folders, magic markered "Stanley Doone." The folders bulged with COMPLAINTS and DEMURRERS, AMENDED COMPLAINTS and ANSWERS, AFFIDAVITS and DECLARATIONS UNDER PENALTY OF PERJURY, MEMORANDA OF POINTS AND AUTHORITIES and MOTIONS TO COMPEL, MINUTE ORDERS and PETITIONS FOR WRITS OF REVIEW. "Try to see things in perspective. What a tribute to the adversarial process your case represents. In these days of slipshod craftsmanship, you might show some respect for dedication. Take it from me, you're never gonna see one battled harder from both ends. These days, it's pretty much make-a-demand, get-an-offer, split-the-baby."

Princeton Gutkin gazed at the bookcase with a pride undiminished by its contents' substance having no more substance than the forecasts of a Chinese cookie. Since he had accepted Tic Myrth's check, Stanley Doone's case had been finished. DONE ... KAPUT ... FINITO ... ... So each responsive pleading was solely his work. Every argument made and rebutted, every authority cited and distinguished, every dispute arisen and resolved his creation. Gutkin had personally researched, drafted, and typed each document. At first, his goal had been simple. Erect a paper fort sturdy enough to deflect Stanley Doone's demands until he raised the cash to satisfy him. Then his efforts had been cursory and schematic. But the more he worked, the more thorough he became. Now he brought to bear every arrow in the Civil Procedurist's quiver. Now he forged propositions as strongly tempered as the fortifications off Omaha Beach, as sharply honed as the pungi sticks sewn into the jungle floor around Quang Tri. Weekly, he reconnoitered law libraries from Palo Alto to Berkeley to buttress the positions he staked.

Princeton Gutkin's absorption in the case had caused him not to care that his actual practice suffered. It mattered more to him now if plaintiff would be allowed use of the driver-agent's deposition, taken before his company-principal had been joined as a party, than that a week's phone messages lay unanswered on his desk. It was more important to decide defendant's fine for refusing inspection of vehicles in their control than that his In-box overflowed, his Out-box stood empty, and Panda sat, word processor dim, engrossed in the collected works of Danielle Steele. It was irrelevant and immaterial that the driver, company, and vehicles existed only in his head.

Doone v. Keep-On Trucking had taken on a life of its own. He thought about it most of his working hours. He dreamed about it nights. His mind continually tugged at the case, making an argument, knocking it down, extending the refashioned argument as far as it would stretch. His own sense of purpose was contingent upon the worth of this work. His reason for being rested on its citation-by-citation ascent into excellence, by the possibility he could achieve something never before known, by the recognition that but-for-Princeton-Gutkin this would not have been.

Beppo, for all his furshlugginer dreaming, could never have pulled off something like this. None of his feeb cousins would ever have a whiff of what he had achieved. He remembered Thanksgiving dinners and Hanukah first nights after which, without fail, the cousins — Stuart and Jonas and Sally and even dopey, pimply Toby — would detach from him and float away with tales of trips to Miami or Bermuda or accounts of dancing class lessons or comparisons of roller skates and Schwinns, as if hoisted upon hot air balloons. And he heard his remarks not fit and he saw himself excluded and he felt himself lack all that it took to belong. Now, when he cracked a corner of the case, it jacked him higher than two martinis at Top of the Mark.

He could not explain the change. It was soothing though. The quiet the research provided and the calm from searching for answers within himself were a relief from his daily pressures. Practicing law had become like walking through a fetid, clamorous alley. His files, with their recitations of old wounds, reeked like garbage sacks. His phone shrieked like a pack of mangy tabbies. His clients, with their incessant demands, had become a gauntlet of maimed, unruly panhandlers, popping out of doorways, pleading for "Spare change." And each day's manipulations seemed to twist him deeper into some darker, narrower, more dangerous passageway that led him further from the placid, spacious, luxurious boulevards, for which he had aimed.

Stanley Doone's case made Princeton Gutkin doubt he would ever get on track. He felt like he had crept and crawled and slithered to some ultimate, unforgiving DEAD END. A massive brick wall like none he had ever encountered stood before him. He could not get over it or under it, and he could not turn around. The wall had a door, but he could not find the key. No matter how thickly his folders swelled, they were no final solution. No matter how brilliantly he impersonated two law firms on paper, he was no vaudeville quick-change artist, who could successfully play both plaintiff and defense attorneys in court, flinging on and off three-piece suits, opening and shutting attache cases, shouting objections to his own questions, while running back and forth between both sides of the counsel table. He could not go to trial. He lacked the funds to settle. He was absolutely stymied.

"I am not criticizing you personally, man. You 'n' Tisa, you've been fucking great. But I'm sure these delays are planned to make me crack." Stanley Doone pushed his glasses up the bridge of his nose. "That sleazy shyster on the other side is fucking with us."

"I'm certain he's simply serving his client as best he can."

"Bullshit, man! Tell him to pay me! Now!" BAM! BAM! BAM! "Fuck! Or I'm taking *him* to the Bar." "I will tell him," Princeton Gutkin said. "But I doubt it will do much good."

JAMES

Chapter VIII.

Jerome Heavens parked his Dodge van at the municipal lot at Fifth and Mission between a steel-blue Toyota Camry and a cherry-red Trans Am with a T-top, gold racing stripes, gold flame-work on its hood. Before he had bought the van from the junker in Pinole, a florist had used it for deliveries. He did a valve job, relined the brakes, painted over everything with black: the name; the number; the three-foot wide American Beauty rose. All he left unpainted was F-L-O-W.

On the floor of the front of the passenger side of the van were sheets of crumpled newspaper, the *Star*, the *News*, the *National Enquirer*; two Colonel Sanders buckets; three Taco Bell trays; a dozen ketchup packets; some styrofoam cups, cigarette holes punched through their bottoms and gouged into their sides. In back were a sleeping bag; a pillow case stuffed with dirty clothes; four Phillip K.Dick paperbacks; a two-year-old issue of *American Hunter*; a beach chair; a Walkman; some Thelonious Monk cassettes; six Chef Boyardee cans; several packs of oyster crackers; a tote bag filled with toiletries; a gold framed photograph of his mother; a rolled up Oriental throw rug; sixteen bottles of aspirins lifted from Pay Less; a hash pipe; two twenty-five-pound dumbbells; a Larry Bird Mikasa; two cartons of bullets for the Walther.

Jerome Heavens put the headset to the Walkman on under his rainbow cap. He put the kit and three cassettes into the pocket of his black jacket with the Walther. He walked down Fifth and turned west on Market. He walked up and down Market for two hours. He walked past stores selling three hundred-fifty purple high-heeled boots and stores selling sweat socks, six pair for two dollars. He walked past mustard pretzels turning on spits and ducks dripping in windows. He walked past a woman pulling a cart filled with rocks and a man laughing at a Yellow Pages cover. He walked past a pit at an abandoned construction site, where people slept in sewer pipes and packing crates. The shelves of the stores reminded him of the floor of his van and the streets of the city, the shelves of the stores.

In such a city, pity did not lie. In it, no prayer could be answered. No rule constrained this city. No punishment dissuaded it. Threats produced nothing. Shame was not a consideration. In such a city, the beaten were kicked. The trampled were stoned. The brightest lights in the city were from those burning on its stakes. The strongest songs were from those strapped upon its racks. What could one say, sacred and professional, to such a city? What did one care? Why should one attempt to distinguish when everything could be answered by the application of the proper match? Why should erasures not begin?

UNESCO Mamas was playing at the Rivoli. Jerome Heavens looked at the glass-encased posters. The black-haired girl licking the chopsticks. The blonde straddling Uncle Sam's stovepipe hat. Neither girl looked like his mother. His mother had green eyes. She had freckles. She wore loose, filmy dresses, on which she sewed stars and half-moons and signs of the zodiac. She would drop a sugar cube laced with acid and turn on Jimi Hendrix and whirl around and around the living room of their cottage. He was not sure why his mother had brought him into this world with its filth and trash and meanness and disease. Why she had left him with his pain. But she had returned and ordained the recommencement of his sacred and professional erasings. When Jerome Heavens noticed the caged cashier staring, he turned away from the photos.

"Pictures of missing gerbils," said the dwarf.

The hot dog stand was not much wider than a phone booth and not much cooler than a Turkish towel. The dwarf with the two-inch aperture in his skull was behind the counter talking to the only customer, an obese woman in lime green acrylic pants and Kelly green t-shirt: YOU'VE GOT A FRIEND IN PENNSYLVANIA. Jerome Heavens sat on the stool furthest from the front and the obese woman. He could see across Market Street to the Plaza and the Medical Arts Building's front door.

"Olivia Newon-John lacks proper security," the woman said. "When I went to call, I was almost molested. I have reported it to all the proper authorities. The governor. The mayor. The chief of police. They all gave me the deaf ear. It has been one of my most heart-rending experiences."

"Two kielbasas," Jerome Heavens said.

"Three guys jump off the Golden Gate Bridge," the dwarf said, coming over to him. "Who's the first one hits the ground? You hear this? A Yid, a spade, a Porto Riccin."

"I don't know," Jerome Heavens said. He sighted the length of the counter at the Medical Arts Building like down a shotgun barrel.

"Who cares."

"That is an awful joke," the woman said. "It is repellant and depressing and morbid and grim. It is hateful and contemptuous and lacking in compassion and redemption and all uplifting value."

"It's democratic," the dwarf said, not looking at her. "It's Equal Opportunity humor. Like if you are talking to a Jew, you can say the one's a Guinea."

"How you know you're talking to a Jew?" Jerome Heavens said.

"You know. What, you don't know who you're talking to?"

"I know."

"Darn right, you know. You know all the time." The wall calendar showed a blue-eyed, blonde girl, tangled in a ball of yarn with a kitten. May 1978, the calendar said. It said that every day of every month of every year while neither girl nor kitten made progress toward escape or strangulation. On either side, a yellowed, crusted strip of fly paper spiraled to the floor. "You read about this TV anchorman back east, Virgil Kipfus? Goes into this hospital with intestine pains. They pull a gerbil out his asshole."

"They what?" Jerome Heavens said.

"A gerbil. Like a hamster. Donchu read the papers? These homos put 'em in plastic baggies with, like, coke and shake 'em up till they are wired. Then they stick 'em up their assholes. Have a real good time." The dwarf plopped the kielbasas on the griddle between the bratwurst and a Coney Island. "Only this guy broke the string on his."

"This another joke you're telling me?"

"No. This ain't no joke. This is reality." The dwarf turned the kielbasas with his tongs. "What's one gerbil say to the other gerbil? That's the joke."

"I don't know."

"'Let's go over Virgil's and get shitface.' You hear Virgil's quitting Channel 8 for a new job?" Jerome Heavens shook his head. The obese woman was tapping her coffee cup on the counter. Her hair was orange and greasy. Four lines ran down one cheek as if someone had clawed her with a fork.

"Yeah, he's moving to New Hamptster. You hear Virg's back in the hospital?" The dwarf turned the kielbasas again. "Having a mole removed."

Jerome Heavens sighted down the counter at the Medical Arts Building's front door. He had not been inside the Medical Arts Building for two weeks. When he was inside the Medical Arts Building, with its NO SMOKING signs, its over-priced pharmacy, its nervous men and women waiting for their X-rays and biopsies and blood cell counts, the receptionist would say, Dr. Chabchap is not in. Can anyone else help you? No, he would say, hating being with the nervous fools, milling like cattle in the slaughter yard. No one else can help me. He slipped a hand into the pocket with the tape cassettes and the Walther. It was time to insist that he see Dr. Chabchap.

"How come you ain't been around?" the dwarf said.

"I been around, I been busy." Jerome Heavens said.

"Everybody's busy. It's the nature of the age." The dwarf slapped the second kielbasa on its bun and wiggled it at Jerome Heavens. "Well, they ought to pay attention. Ten-hour days can cripple you like cancer. Commuting on the Bayshore will kill you dead as strychnine."

"I pay attention." Jerome Heavens put mustard, ketchup, relish, diced onion, two helpings of sauerkraut on each kielbasa. He rolled them in wax paper and lay them in a paper bag. There had been two hundred sixty-two in the register and thirty-one more in the wallet of the mantis. The toad-woman had a turquoise ring. He paid for the kielbasas without tipping.

"When Olivia left me for John Travolta, it broke my heart," the obese woman said. "She was such a precious spirit. I hoped he would be kind to her. I prayed he would be as gentle and as sweet as kind. It was the only dream by which I had to abide."

"Hey, I almost forgot," yelled the dwarf. "What are they putting on jars of vaseline these days?"

Jerome Heavens ate his kielbasas on a concrete bench on the second tier of the plaza, directly facing the entrance to the Medical Arts Building. A line of pigeons perched on the railing, level with his eye. A man in a salmon-colored leisure suit bore an eight-foot wooden cross back and forth in front of the BART entrance below. Another man beat a trap drum and a third shook a tambourine to attract donations from the commuters, as if the cross-bearer's effort was insufficient alone. When he finished eating, Jerome Heavens lit a joint of sinsemilla with a kitchen match.

The people he hated most of the people walking in and out of the Medical Arts Building were the pregnant women. He hated how they leaned clumsily against the wall. He hated the sweat blotching their faces. Most of all, he hated that they carried within more creatures which would increase the filth and trash and disease. These creatures would suck blood and food and money from the women. In return, they would poison the women's world. The stupid women. His mother would have never permitted herself to become a woman like those. The pregnant women reminded him of the caterpillars on whose backs the flies laid eggs which, when hatched, fed on and killed the caterpillars whose bodies had succored them. He remembered when he would drop a caterpillar on a nest of black ants in the fields around the Community; and the ants would swarm over the huge, soft, pulpy, squirming body and nibble it dead.

He swung the wheel of the Walkman to ten. He could hear the theme in every note of Monk's solo: strike; release; and pause. He could hear the theme in every phrase: tone; timbre; and speed. He could hear the humor and the agony, the amusement and the sorrow, the eternal war between the order and the madness. Each note related to each phrase, and each phrase was shaped for each song, and each song related to every other song and the phrases and notes in each of them. He admired the way the notes stumbled and staggered and fell without the pace or progression or juxtaposition that would have achieved beauty and sense for any average man. He felt he understood Monk's vision better than any average one.

He realized how good the dope was when the music no longer interested him. All that interested him was what was going on inside his head. He realized something was going when he sensed his self floating above his body, in front of it and to the right. This arrangement seemed sensible and correct. In this way, the body could act without exposing the self to risk. The body could go places and have experiences and collect data for this hovering self to process and bring to consciousness and convey to him — him-him — Jerome Heavens-him — what was there and how it felt and who, even, he was.

All he was, he realized, was what his mind permitted him to be. What it allowed him to experience from the collected data — the sights and sounds and smells — the dripping ducks and Monk runs and grease sizzling on the dwarf's griddle. And a mind did not catch that much. It missed the molecules and impulses, the sound waves and color gradations that composed what it did perceive. It missed the histories behind these perceptions, the explanations and forces that accounted for their being. It missed the consequences that would result from any decisions he made because of what he thought it had recognized. And since all these perceptions were composed of impulses and did have histories and consequences, his mind was delivering him no more of this ocean than any faulty sieve.

He liked this thinking. It felt too solid to be damaged by any little thing. Like not tipping. Or stealing two hundred sixty-two dollars. Or shooting someone in the eye. Even when you thought you were perceiving an event fully, you were missing so much more. The history behind the person you shot. The consequences of shooting him. That he and you were only impulses and chemicals.

He liked thinking everyone was impulses. That made dying only matter breaking down. The flesh decayed. The bones crumbled. The chemicals dissolved. All that remained were the impulses, electric waves, released like a Monk chord into the cosmos, beating on. His mother was out there, whirling and spinning in the cosmos as if across the cottage floor. He would join her soon. He did not know how impulses made contact, but he believed it would satisfy.

The mind made things so delightful. Nothing could be more delightful than sitting on this bench, having thoughts like these. There was no point to any other thing. Even if his mother was beside him, he would not tell her what he was thinking. That would be a concession to coming back from where he was. He would rather remain there forever, risking no part of his body or self, reveling in the construct of his mind's delightful thoughts.

But — the thought suddenly coursed through him — striking like a fire-poker on a small boy's hand — biting like teeth through flesh and cartilage and bone — if his reality depended on what his mind levered conscious from what it did perceive, wasn't he utterly at risk? Couldn't his mind cloak him in the terrible as tightly as the delightful? Abide in the excruciating as totally as the divine? Wouldn't a mind attach to pain instead of pleasure if that mind preferred pain? Or if someone else controlled that mind and twisted it in that fashion?

He remembered the woman who lived in the bus stop shelter on Upper Grant with the lice in her hair. He remembered the man in the Tuffy garbage bag, pounding his hands bloody, screaming "Harder! Harder!" at the wall. He remembered the boy on the gurney, wheeled into the E.R. at General, who had taken the razor and sliced off his cock. Someone had thrown the switch that fried their minds and reduced them to swill.

The man bearing the cross was producing scanty change for his companions. The one thrashed his tambourine. The other flailed his drum. The commuters passed them with embarrassment or fear. The blackest pigeon on the rail huffed and ruffled its feathers. Its head was black, its wings; blackness rimmed the pigeon's orange claw. Jerome Heavens dug his nails into his palms to stop his thinking. He clamped his molars on the linings of his cheeks. The patients would be gone by now. Dr. Chabchap would see him.

Look him in the eye.

JACK KATZ © 2016

Chapter IX.

"I hardly see you any more," Tisa Rio said. "You're always running off to some library." "The statute of limitations is giving me trouble," Princeton Gutkin said, "in Stanley Doone's case. But it may be tolled as long as the co-defendant was out of state." "Lucky Stanley Doone." Tisa Rio had both elbows on the rose marble table, the rinds of a quartered grapefruit on her plate, a cup of coffee in both hands. She wore lilac Reebok high tops, daisy yellow spandex legwarmers, a black Esprit t-shirt, French cut. She watched Princeton Gutkin make a note on the inch-square, gummy-backed yellow pad next to his napkin ring. He tore off the top slip and stuck it in his shirt pocket. He kept inch-square, gummy-backed note pads everywhere now: beside the bed; behind the toilet; on the dashboard of his Porsche. He had eaten half of one of his fried eggs, one of his four sausage links, one bite from his four slices of sour dough toast. All his shirts came back from the laundry with steamed yellow slips of paper crinkled up in pockets.

"Lucky all right. It hit me, I was looking in the mirror, ready to shave. Schmuck, I thought. You haven't checked common law precedent. I'm heading for Boalt Hall to start with Australia."

"Fascinating."

"It's amazing when you think about it. One minute, I don't have a clue. I'm standing there, scraping foam off my upper lip. My mind's blank. The next minute, there're possibilities."

"Like a message from God."

"Exactly."

"Like he was talking to you from inside a can of Colgate Mentholated." Princeton Gutkin looked at his eggs.

"Well, bon voyage!" She flung her cup at the sink.

"Tisa!"

"And when you're not running to some library, all you want is to play Scrabble. Scrabble, for God's sake. I guess I should be grateful it's not Candyland."

"Interesting game, Scrabble." Princeton Gutkin bent to pick up the pieces of the cup. She could see the bald spot at the crown of his head. The sag of his belly over his belt. She watched him lift each piece gingerly, so he would not nick the fingers that had to scribble notes on the tiny yellow pads. "Very educational. You gain command of a lot of sharp words to use in important situations. Drafting briefs. Drafting pleadings. The right word in the right place can make all the difference."

"I don't draft pleadings. In case you haven't noticed, I don't draft flippin' briefs." Tisa Rio stared out the window at the cloudless sky. It was one of those perfect San Francisco mornings. In every charcuterie on Union Street, a Doctor's Wife from Pacific Heights would be at the counter with her baguettes and goat cheese, telling another Doctor's Wife, "I could see the Farallones." Whatever the hell the Farallones were. Wherever the hell they were. As long as she had been in San Francisco, she would not know a Farralone if one bit her on the tit. "Do you know the last time we made love?"

"I've had a lot on my mind, baby."

"Two weeks ago last Thursday. You came in forty-five seconds." "I didn't know you had a stopwatch on me. This some kind of Olympic trials?" "I don't even know why you want me around. I'm serious, Princeton. I bet you'd have more fun with the O.E.D. It'd teach you a lot more words than I could; and whenever you got horny, hon, you could open to whichever got you hot and whack away." "You're important to me, baby. I like you very much. Everybody likes you. Just yesterday, Stanley Doone was telling me how crazy he is about you." "Fuck Stanley Doone."

"Stanley Doone is an important client, keep in mind."

Princeton Gutkin had returned to the table. Tisa Rio could not see his bald spot, but she knew it was there, growing bigger, like his belly was growing bigger, as though the weight of his sagging belly was stretching his scalp wide. She watched him cut an egg with his fork and place the piece in his mouth. She liked thinking that the egg was cold, the yolk congealed, and that it had to taste like the financial section.

"It's smart business to make nice to important clients. His case is worth a bundle to you and me." "I can be nice to important clients. But why can't you have important clients who are chairmen of the board or chief executive officers like Moses Weinreb?" "Mo has an entirely different practice than me. You handle corporate acquisitions, you're gonna have clients with daughters at the Conservatory, be able to discuss Krishnamurti, know which is the salad fork. You do P.I., you're lucky they don't use it to pick their nose." "But Stanley Doone ... You could, at least, stop inviting him over." "Stanley Doone is an educated man. With fascinating ideas. You make an effort, you could enjoy his company." "I don't want to enjoy his company. I want to enjoy your company. We're never alone any more. I'm totally serious. Either you're at some library or you're with Stanley Doone." "We're alone now."

"Your pants are here. Your Fruit of the Looms. Your peter's halfway to Boalt Hall. Dr. Chumus thinks my demands for intimacy make you fear the loss of your penis. For protection, you have withdrawn from me."

"Hellova sharp fellow, Chumus. Talk about your dollars well spent. Sometimes, I think I've been neglecting the social sciences in my research. Maybe I should range afield. Take an interdisciplinary approach. Some of the issues I've raised practically call for a Brandeis Brief."

Tisa Rio counted silently to herself. She got to "three" before Princeton Gutkin tore another slip of paper from the note pad. "Why don't we go away. Take a vacation. The two of us."

"Things are a little tight at the office."

"We don't have to go for long. A couple days. An inn up the coast for a long weekend. Hot springs. Mud baths. Catch some rays. I'm totally serious, hon. If we pack the cooler with dry ice, the Readi-Whip will keep."

"Sounds terrific. But I'm jammed. I have depositions lined up all month on ..." "... on the Doone case."

"... the Doone case. Exactly."

"*Princeton*! I am seriously worried about you. It is not just sex or Scrabble or Stanley Doone." Tisa Rio had pulled her chair next to his. She pushed the *Chronicle* at him. "This city is going crazy. Check it out."

OCCULT SHOP KILLINGS, the four column headline said.

"I know that store," Princeton Gutkin said.

"I know it too. It's around the corner from your office. You go by it every day. Shoot, doesn't it make you feel weird? Like hellish things are closing in."

"I go by it every day."

"I *know* you go by that store. I *said* you go by it. *Princeton*, aren't you listening? Don't you think it's like an omen? Like some noose is tightening?"

"It looks strictly workers' comp, though." Princeton Gutkin ran a finger down the page. "You get snuffed on the job, the insurance pays a set sum to the dependents. No dependents, the money goes to the state. You can't go against the company direct. You can't get more than the law says. People getting killed at work's a fixed cost of business the employer writes off. Thanks for thinking of me, babe; but that's no way to make a nickel."

§

After Princeton Gutkin had left, Tisa Rio spread her mat on the floor of the second bedroom. The second bedroom had no bed. It had a rowing machine, a stationary bike, a pull-up bar, an incline board, a set of shiny chrome weights, a padded bench, two blue director's chairs. Princeton had tried the rowing machine once, before claiming aggravation of a war wound. He had done a half mile on the bike and spent forty minutes soaking in the tub. She opened the blinds, turned up the heat, slapped a Bob Seger in the CD at full volume.

Tisa Rio *loved* exercise. She believed in total health. "*Mens sana*," she would tell Princeton, "in the, you know, *corpore sano*." One day, when she was on his case about being such a slug, he had tried to bring her down by claiming the Greeks liked boys. She had stripped, done fifty side-straddle hops, and left him tripping over his *schlong*. She worked out one hour every morning, studying the programs of older, wiser fitness enthusiasts — Raquel Welch, Jane Fonda, Christie Brinkley — to formulate her own.

Who wants to ride that chrome three-wheeler?
Who wants to make that first mistake?
Who wants to wear those gypsy leathers
And head out to Fire Lake?

"Huh-hu-hu." For five minutes, she hopped from one foot to another, curling, one at a time, a two-pound dumbbell in each hand. It was fantastic aerobically. It was fantastic spiritually too. It burned the gunk from your head. A good sweat could really make you see yourself. Who you were and where your journey had taken you and where you still could go. "Vhr-vr-vr." She snapped both arms above her head, stiff-elbowed, then drove them down behind her, bending forward from the waist. It was fantastic, she thought, to have journeyed from uptight Sulfleur Pond to Princeton's penthouse. From her parents' *Brady Bunch* ranch house, with its green picket fence, its color TV on twenty-four seven; her father's softball trophies, her mother's ceramic Jesuses, her brother, Eddie, Jr., crashed in the basement with his fat wife Faye and their two fat kids, Roni and Eddie, III, collecting Health and Welfare, waiting for the Goodyear plant's reopening. From having to take serious her father and mother and the Sisters at St. Elaina Maria Theresa's carping and complaining and trying to scare her into thinking she was damned for trying to plug more choices into her life than whether her picket fence was green or white, whether she settled for four channels or added cable and got forty-two, whether or not she married some other Eddie, Jr., who'd end up in *his* parents' basement crushing beer cans in one paw. "Fhh-fh-fh." Tisa Rio dipped her knees and jabbed and hooked the dumbbells at imaginary enemies. It was far out to think she would not hear them any more.

With Princeton's taste in music, though, she might as well be at her parents. Beatles. Stones. One or two Bruce Springsteens. Thank God, she had found Bob Seger. He had been a favorite since she was small. She hoped she would never get tired of him. It was reassuring to have someone you always loved. She did not think she would get tired of Bob Seger, even if she had got tired of Bruce. Bruce could be so gloomy. So depressing.

Such a drag sometimes. "Frr-fr-fr." Tisa Rio crouched and straightened, crouched and straightened, swinging both dumbbells behind her, as if preparing to dive. Bruce loved rock 'n' roll; but there were all those dark roads and rainy nights and lonely, achy rides he was always running into. "Ssh-sh-sh." She bent from side-to-side at the waist, rocking back and forth across her pelvis, extending each dumbbell toward the floor. But with Bob Seger, rock 'n' roll was enough. Rock 'n' roll blasted everything away. It was like Bob Seger had this commitment to rock 'n' roll, like she had her commitment to hauling her ass out of Sulfleur Pond; and if you held onto your commitment, it blasted other stuff away.

And, *God,* what was wrong with Princeton? He was such a drag. Such an old lady. Princeton was really on the rag these days. "Rhh-rh-rh." Tisa Rio jumped into the air a hundred times, curling and releasing a dumbbell with each jump, alternating hands. Princeton never used to worry about money. He never used to be tied up in one case. Cases had been pieces of property for Princeton. You wheeled and dealed and partied off the profits till it was time to cash another one. Now he had this Stanley Doone he might as well be married to. "Vrr-vr-vr." She jumped a hundred times more, pressing a dumbbell to her shoulder on the first jump, pressing it overhead on the second, bringing it down in two stages on the third and fourth, repeating with the other arm. If Princeton was so worried and so involved, there must be more money in the case than in any other he ever had. There must be so much money that, if it was yours, it would set you up for life. If you had a commitment to hauling your ass out of places you had outgrown, that would be the kind of case to have. She jumped a hundred times, beginning with her arms extended outward at her sides, then clanging the dumbbells together in front of her chest as if applauding her thinking.

Tisa Rio sank into a director's chair. She was sweating hard. She was breathing fast. She did nothing but let her sweat pour and her heart race. When the CD stopped, she did not replace it. *God,* she loved exercising. She could be tired or bored, and, inside an hour, she could be totally clear. She was aware of herself and nothing but herself and the nature of her journey. It was she who had gotten herself out of Sulfleur Pond. She felt proud and accomplished and capable of achieving all goals. She was fleshing out the woman she was meant to be.

She was touching herself with one hand. She had not planned it. It happened now and then. She put the other hand on her breast. It was happening more with Princeton busy with Stanley Doone. It felt nice but she would not let it get too far. She did not want to encourage the habit. It was hard to stop because it felt good. Dr. Chumus would not mind. Dr. Chumus believed in the person's right to positive feelings. Dr. Chumus provided guidance to stripping away the old and revealing the new. She rubbed herself faster. Dr. Chumus — Chester Chumus — had brown eyes, a curly beard, the cutest chunky body. She was wet now. She could feel the tingle in her breasts and tummy. She saw Chester kick off his Birkenstocks, bounce out of his stressless chair toward her, upset his herbal tea.

"Unh-uh-uh." Tisa Rio felt herself negativity free. She could not believe how totally she had escaped Sulfleur Pond. She remembered the morning, the summer after graduating high school, she had realized she had nothing to do. Not nothing to do but get high with Pidgie Blumberg and veg out by the pool, soaking up UVs. Not nothing to do but turn on with Chipper Geyser and ball in the back of his 'Bago. Nothing-nothing to do. She had walked around the house in her bra and panties, nibbling a cherry TastyKake. In the den, she pulled the family photo albums from the shelf. There she was. Maid of honor at Eddie and Faye's wedding. Arms linked with Mickey and Goofy at DisneyWorld. *En pointe*, at age ten, as a Sugarplum Fairy. Nothing in the past to make her think her future would go "Wow!" She had dressed and filled her backpack and headed out the door for Trailways, like some dumb Made-for-TV movie, starring her as some dumb problem child.

From the second she had hit San Francisco, she had known she had made the right choice. San Fran was loaded with potentialities for joy and growth. She could not open her mail without finding a catalogue from some Center for Alternative Study that promised her awareness more scope. She could not pass a poster tree without spotting a flyer that guaranteed a more actualized self. But even this had not satisfied her. She could not keep from feeling bitchy each time she was reminded that not one moment of satori could be cashed at the Quik Stop for steak and beer. That no matter how often she chanted her mantra, it remained insufficient deposit for a flat in the Golden Gateway. She had been living in a commune in the Panhandle she had found through a *Bay Guardian* classified — no meat, no alcohol, no sex — the atmosphere as high as it was confining — the New Age as uptight as New Jersey — when along came Princeton — Mr. Swinging Single with his buffed nails, La Costa tan, silver-haired as Johnny Carson.

Tisa Rio walked to the window. She still saw nothing on the horizon. She felt bad that Princeton did not have time to pursue his own fulfillment; but, maybe, he was at this place where hard work was what he was committed to. She could respect that; she could give him space because, really, that commitment was in harmony with hers. Because hard work produced the money to keep Sulfleur Pond away. And Sulfleur Pond was always out there — like Bruce's dark nights and lonely roads — always waiting for you to give up, like Faye and Eddie, Jr. had given up and crawled back into her parents' basement, so it could suck you down. It was like the tar pits in those picture books in grade school. The wooly mammoths got stuck; and the sabertooths, attracted by their bellows, pounced upon their backs; and the vultures landed on the roaring sabertooths; and all of them were too busy chewing one another to know the tar pit had them all sucked down.

Stanley Doone's case seemed worth enough money to keep Sulfleur Pond away for a long time. She was centered now, and she could see that. If Princeton worked hard, they would get their share. If Princeton did not, Stanley would get another lawyer; and what would keep Sulfleur Pond away then? This made Tisa Rio feel better about Princeton's hard work, but it bugged her. She did not like that what happened to her depended upon decisions by Stanley Doone and that Stanley's decisions depended upon actions by Princeton. And she did not have to be dependent. She was attractive and intelligent and — Princeton was right — well liked by

Stanley Doone. She could be helpful in her way.

Tisa Rio punched the buttons on the Princess phone.

"I'm-uh not here." The speed with which Stanley's voice came on suggested he must be afraid to give a caller time to reconsider having dialed and hang up. "But there is this machine."

It also irritated her, come to think of it, that, no matter how hard Princeton worked and no matter how friendly she was, Stanley Doone would keep two-thirds of the money.

"Hey, Stanley, it's Tisa. Want to get together for a bite?"

§

Princeton Gutkin sat on a folded towel on the lower of two slatted benches in his health club's sauna. His back rested against the upper tier. His feet rested on one of the planks, which fenced off the metallic, copper-colored, artificial coal-topped brazier which heated the sauna. He stared at the coals, inhaled the heat, and hoped that a good burn would rejuvenate his thinking.

He had been unable to research Australian common law. At Boalt Hall's circulation desk, he had felt his heart pound and his chest tighten. Too many books could do that to a guy. You could only eyeball so much ink into your head before your body told you to get back to life and quit ducking. At law school, where values had been set by feebs who measured life's worth by tenths of grade point averages, it was easy for an otherwise red-blooded American boy to sink into a library carrel and never emerge, all his juice pressed into petrification by stacks of Blackstone's *Commentaries* and *AmJur* 2nd. Then, when he'd played the game too long, he would end up in some bar, chugging several cans of Miller's, calling all *Review*-types "Asshole," punching out a window, puking in the john. Now, his research and drafting were designed to avoid confronting Stanley Doone. But Stanley Doone could not be avoided. The crumb was a clear and present threat. The proper method for self-assertion was less apparent than when he was in law school, but the danger of his extinction more severe.

The other man in the sauna was Nicholas Phillipoulos, a criminal defense attorney, who was, as the cognoscenti put it, "well connected downtown." Nicholas Phillipoulos had been Phi Bait at St. Mary's, studied Kant on a Danforth at Oxford, and come back to Stanford Law. He spent two years in the S.F.P.D.'s office, then gone solo, ascending from the representation of Hunter's Point muggers to Rodeo crack manufacturers to Portola Valley residents, who referred to one another as "Chicken Gizzard," "Big Vanilla," and "Timmy the Pipe" and, according to a recently leaked F.B.I. Wiretap, their counselor as "Nickie Books."

The good news for attorneys who represented such clients was that they generally had funds to pay for services. The bad news was the nature of the services those clients often required. Nicholas Phillipoulos lived on a ranch in Danville with his wife Giulliana, a modern dancer from Mills, and two children, Ariel and Achilles, who attended The Etruscan School. Nicholas and Giulliana, who had waist-length blonde hair, and whom Princeton Gutkin once observed, at a reception for the Attorney General, crouched beneath a Steinway grand, weeping into her plate of Thai barbecue, raised Arabians, spent two months each summer abroad, were on the boards of the Berkeley Film Festival, the Clarence Darrow Foundation, and I Ching House. Nicholas Phillipoulos was also, Gutkin assumed, at leisure on a Wednesday morning because of the eight count federal indictment, which had followed the leaked wiretaps, referring to his bank accounts in Grand Cayman, the landing strip and four cargo planes he had purchased for cash, and the bloodstains in the trunk of his Silver Shadow that corresponded to those of the missing Secret Witness Program stalwart, Apollo "Ten Thumbs" Abbondondo.

"Fucking club," Nicholas Phillipoulos said, slapping down his *Chronicle*.

"They give it the good try," Princeton Gutkin said.

"I walked into a stall this morning. Two turds floating in the bowl." Princeton Gutkin eyed the paper. He had wondered what would be on the mind of someone whose contemplations had progressed in a few decades from the abstractions of *A Critique of Pure Reason* to the reality of the new seizure statutes, by which the feds could walk off with the entire north forty, all the ponies, the kids' crested blazers, Giulliana's sweaty Danskins. He felt neither repelled by nor condemnatory of Nicholas Phillipoulos. He felt, instead, a kinship with and curiosity about someone who, like himself, hungered to load his plate with double portions. Plus, if accounts were to be believed, Nickie Books had a scoop or two of *crème fraiche* on him. Gutkin felt they were like two foreign agents rendezvousing in the sauna and the *Chron* a pack of secrets encoded for exchange.

"Help yourself," Nicholas Phillipoulos said. "Nothing in there's worth a shit. It's all every day. The Prez wants two hundred fifty billion to put a laser fence around the lower forty-eight, destroy unfriendly in-comings and keep out Mexicans. The Guv's encouraging Dick and Jane to drop a dime on mom and dad for smoking weed, cheating on their taxes, not buckling up when they drive to Little League. And the Supremes have clarified what part of your anatomy you can rub against who else's without drawing hard time."

Princeton Gutkin picked up the newspaper.

Before he could look at it, Nicholas Phillipoulos said, "Who did 'Singing the Blues'?" "Excuse me?"

"'Singing the Blues.' You know. 'Never-felt-more-like-crying-all-night. Cause-everything's-wrong. Nothing-ain't-right ...' I'll give you a hint. Gee-you-why."

"Madison?" Princeton Gutkin said.

"Uh-uh. Mitchell." Nicholas Phillipoulos had heavy lids, a hooked nose, wattles of flesh beneath his neck. He settled back against the walls of the sauna like an iguana on a rock. "I was up all night trying to think of that. All I could come up with was Guy-something. The song was very big at certain parties I was at in the eighth grade."

"Guy Mitchell. I think you're right."

"Fucking-A, I'm right. White guy. Middle-of-the-road. Did 'There's a Pawnshop on a Corner in Pittsburgh, Pennsylvania.' This was his big rock career move. If it was a College Board question, it would be *'Dungaree Doll'-colon. Eddie Fisher. 'Singing the Blues'-colon. Blank.* The choices would be '*Gogi Grant, Don Cherry, The Four Lads, Guy Mitchell.*'"

"Guy Mitchell," Princeton Gutkin said.

"Now this one is really obscure. To answer this, you have to be one hundred percent on the bus." Princeton Gutkin took a deep breath.

"Those parties were always in some chick's rec room. Pine paneling. Bowls of pretzels on the wet bar. The ping pong table folded up and rolled away. The guys wore white button down shirts over black turtlenecks. The girls wore crew neck sweaters with circle pins on their Peter Pan collars. You remember those parties?"

"Sure."

"We started making out at them. Seventh grade was Post Office and Spin the Bottle. Eighth was flip off the lights and go for second base, third, handfuls of bare ass. Man, I used to throw erections just walking in the door. 'Good evening, Nicholas.' 'Good evening, Mrs Taconelli, Mr. Taconelli.' SPROING! They didn't jump out of the way, my peter'd pin them to the wall. So, now, one other song I associate with those parties. For sixty-four thousand dollars, what? First thing in your mind."

Princeton Gutkin had been listening hard. Outside the sauna, a locker slammed. He felt like Nicholas Phillipoulos had always been two days ahead of him. Had turned into the same twisted alley. Crawled down the same dark passageway. Slithered up to the same brick wall. But, somehow, Nickie Books had busted through.

"'Green Door,'" he heard himself say.

"'Green Door!'" Nicholas Phillipoulos yelled.

The air had rushed out of Princeton Gutkin in the half second between his answer and Nicholas Phillipoulos' response. It rushed back and he was full.

"'There's-a-something-something-and-a-something-something,'" Nicholas Phillipoulos sang, "'Behind-the-green-door.'" "'Green door,'" Princeton Gutkin sang, "'What's-that-secret-you're-keeping?'" "I don't remember any more words," Nicholas Phillipoulos said. "I don't remember if a guy sang it or a girl or group. I just remember it from those parties." "On *Your Hit Parade*, it would be Snookie Lanson doing

'Singing the Blues' and Gisele MacKenzie 'Green Door.'" "You got it. Gizzle fucking-MacKenzie. And, man, those magic parties. One time, Mary Lou Collander stuck her hand in my fly, and I shot a load all over my pants. I walked around the rest of the night with my shirt tied around my waist like it was the latest style in '*Playboy* Advisor.'"

Inside the *Chronicle* was a story about a man who had stormed into a doctor's office brandishing a gun. When he was told the doctor was on leave, the man fired two shots into the ceiling and fled. Princeton Gutkin read the story several times. The words sparked like brush fires inside his frontal lobe. His consciousness careened across the sentences as though it had bought a ticket to Crack-the-Whip. The sweat beaded on his face and dribbled down his chest onto his paunch. The paper was dry and brittle from the sauna. He felt he had to memorize the story before it crumbled in his hands.

The doctor's name was Esubio Chabchap.

"Jim Lowe," Nicholas Phillipoulos said. "How's that sound? I just scoped back to eighth grade. Jim Lowe. Un-be-fucking-lievable! He never did anything again."

MAN MURDERS SELF AND FAMILY
BONE
DISEASE
Ariel

Chapter X.

"... for a bite."

Stanley Doone re-wound the tape again. He must have played the message fifty times since the evening before. He had bought the answering machine so Princeton Gutkin could not claim he had returned his calls at times he was not in. In the three weeks he had owned it, the only messages his answering machine had collected had been one from his dentist reminding him that he was nine months late for a cleaning, one from a phone-calling machine offering him a free barbecue set if he would visit a ski chalet time-share near Incline Village, and one from his batty Aunt Faith in Concrete, Washington. "Hello!" his machine had recorded Aunt Faith shrieking. "Hel-lo! Curtis, he's got one of those awful machines. Hel-lo! Hel-lo! Does this mean I have to pay for this call? C-L-I-C-K."

The answering machine was the only thing new in Stanley Doone's apartment. He had a grease-encrusted stove; a graying refrigerator; an army cot with a battered two-drawer chest slid under it; two mismatched folding chairs; a card table, whose oil cloth cover announced: DREAM TIME. His clothes hung from a brass rod screwed to the back of his door. His desk was a wood slab lain across cinder blocks. The only light came from a sixty-watt bulb in the ceiling. The only window faced into an air shaft, surrounded by five additional stories — four above, one below — of the Blue Horizon Residential Hotel. The only decorations were his favorite childhood comic books, preserved in plastic, thumb tacked to walls, flaunting their lurid covers. A severed arm clung to a subway strap. A multi-tentacled, gelatinous blob menaced a scantily clad maiden. A puzzled wife stared at the coffin beneath the Christmas tree while, behind her, her grinning husband swung an axe.

Stanley Doone did not care that his furnishings were old. It did not matter how many previous tenants had pounded wet dreams into his mattress, broken wind upon his chairs, tossed their toenail clippings on his threadbare rug. His apartment satisfied his needs. Stacks of newspapers sat in one corner. Shoe boxes filled with index cards, to which were stapled articles clipped from the newspapers, climbed one wall. Rows of notebooks, containing thoughts and sketches triggered by the clippings, trooped along the floor. And through the air, stitching the 'fridge and cot and comics together, were the clothes-pinned pages, his distillations from the clipped and stapled, the triggered and sketched.

The articles recounted tragedies and calamities and human beings who could not cope. There was the story of the minister in Dayton with fourth stage cancer who locked himself in his garage, connected a hose to the exhaust, and let his Accord run. The fumes seeped into his house and slew his wife and retarded daughter. There was the Time-Warner executive whose divorced son constantly threatened suicide. One day, the executive handed the son a pistol and dared him to pull the trigger. One year later, the father followed suit with the same gun. His wife kept both their ashes on the mantlepiece in East Hampton. There was the child born with the weakened bones. Pick her up, she broke an arm. Make her laugh, there went a rib. The grisly, surprise cause-and-effect seemed to Stanley Doone the work of a sensibility more suited for Roadrunner cartoons than Creative-fucking-Design. The stories were so heart-ripping horrific, so tear duct-draining appalling, they could only be faced if you clamped shut your pre-conditioned mind and laughed. The stories told of those who had met existence's unmitigated truth — the fucked-up and the fucked. They demonstrated, beyond doubt, that no supportive system known to man was worth jack shit.

The insights Stanley Doone had gained from his clippings and developed in his notebooks nested, fully developed, in his portfolios. In the newspapers, the stories had been obscured by the doses of war and flood and famine by which the media anaesthetized their readers into a narcoleptic funk, a blitz of undifferentiated dunderings, as soothing in their way as any de-balled Wyndham Hill elevator jive. Only he had recognized the worth of these stories. Only he had seen they could be plucked from this souk, spun into lightening by the mind and pen, and hurled like epiphianic fire storms to star-burst shatter the deaf-blind, contemporary night. Only his vision could dazzle-jolt, purge-redeem the people.

Readers would hear his words and rend their garments. Viewers would contemplate his pictures and pull an entire sack cloth-ashes trip. Stanley Doone could sit for hours, riveted by the workings out required to make this come down. He had to decide which of the many stories nominated by his clippings merited enshrinement in *Lunacies and Failures.* He had to derive from the few names and facts of the stories full characters, auditioning them on his sketch pad, trotting out and casting away facial expressions, body types, and manners of dress. He had to outline each narrative, decide the number of pages it required, and break each of these pages into panels. He had to consider, not only the content of each panel, but its border, lighting, and the perspective from which it would be viewed. He had to situate his word balloons and captions and select a style for every letter. He had to shape and position each completed panel, so that it worked in conjunction with every other panel on the page — and so each page added to the impact of each volume, and each volume made irresistible the effect of his entire work. He had to seize his readers' eyes and ears and dictate how they scanned his images and received his words, assuring the achievement of his desired end. Until now, as long as his apartment had held his newspapers and cards, his notebooks and portfolios, other considerations had less impact upon him than the nips of its fleas.

In one moment, though, he would be leaving. The purpose filled him with anxiety. Stanley Doone had not been on a date since Leola Minsky had dissolved into hysterics when he slipped and landed — SMACK! SPLAT! — while bringing her a gin fizz at a Fine Arts Department mixer his second semester at San Francisco State. Leola had left twenty minutes later with her faculty advisor, a conceptualist known for the ceramic excrement with which he had place-matted the Board of Supervisors' dais before a meeting of the Budget Committee; and Stanley had spent the remainder of the evening in the men's room, leering at the wolf deck of a Fulbright Scholar from Pakistan. That night had seemed to summarize his relations with women. They were alluring but dangerous. Exciting but treacherous. Lingering in the men's room, the naked blondes, brunettes and redheads fanned for viewing in the Paki's hands, Stanley had recalled the fates of bitches like Leola in his comic books. The one char-broiled and the one quick-frozen and the one whose face had been ripped from her cranial bones.

It had been a dozen years.

Now he had accepted Tisa's invitation to lunch.

Stanley Doone knew about "lunches" like this. They meant secret meetings; whispered, behind-curtain deals; undercover power brokerings; illicit, uninhibited fun. He felt as capable of the experience as anyone. His work had expanded his thinking and enlightened his viewpoint so that "lunch" with him would be more illuminating and broadening than with any of the dim and narrow, conventional types he observed, set out like crystal goblets on white linen tablecloths, in Financial District boites. He had expected to have awaited publication of *Lunacies and Failures* for his social calendar to have begun to fill.

He was glad it was happening.
He was ready for rewards.
For the days dwindle down
To a precious few,
September, November ...

Walter Huston hauntingly sang on Mr. Rabie's victrola next door. Mr. Rabie, seventy-five, wall-eyed, and with two artificial hips, was president of the Blue Horizon's Tenants Association. He played "September Song" at any time of day or night. Sometimes, he played it all day and all night and threw Old Overholt bottles against the wall. The following morning, he placed the broken glass in shopping bags outside his door. The other tenants, primarily pensioners and Social Security recipients, whose own afflictions made Stanley Doone believe he was the only resident of the Blue Horizon who ambulated without the help of Joie de Vivre Orthopedic Appliances or could speak two consecutive sentences without muttering the words "by-pass" or "remission," had elected Mr. Rabie to three consecutive terms.

Stanley Doone closed the door on his apartment. The hall reeked of meatloaf dinners from last night, for tomorrow and today. He wore a brown cableknit sweater under his fatigue jacket. The sweater had a hole which could not be seen if he buttoned his jacket tight. It felt ironic that the blow which had nearly ended his life had provided this shot at revitalization. He could remember the truck. The gaping grill. The beaked hood. A woman had screamed. He had looked and there it was: towering; roaring; close; and fucking steaming. He had not told the police, the doctors, or, even, Princeton Gutkin; but there, also, it was not. He suspected that, if he had taken one more step, the truck would have missed him. He suspected, too, he'd had time for that step. But at the moment he had left the curb, as for many moments over many weeks before, his mind had been hamstrung by a series of lacerating thoughts. What if he never finished *Lunacies and Failures*? Finished but was not published? Was published but not read? Was read but reviled? He had worked without success so long he could not escape thinking he might never grab any. The weight of those questions had held him in place when the woman screamed. His chosen path had led him to that spot in the crosswalk as it led him each morning to his desk. He would betray neither choice by bolting. He was prepared for anything that his dedication earned. He felt unsullied by his silent fraud.

Coach and Mrs. Kopolwitz hobbled off the elevator. Each pulled an identical wagon. Clear plastic tubing ran from a tank on each wagon to their nostrils. Mrs. Kopolwitz often gave Stanley Doone socks her husband had rejected as too floppy or too tight. Coach Kopolwitz often waylaid him with opinions on designated hitters and crack-back blocks. Both Coach and Mrs. Kopolwitz reported to him the latest accomplishments of their son, some slick Hollywood asshole — "A producer, a director, a writer, Stanley, like you" — with the glee of someone sticking needles into dolls.

Pumps drove something through the tubes that made it worthwhile for Coach and Mrs. Kopolwitz to keep pulling their wagons.

"Good morning, Stanley. Lovely day," Mrs. Kopolwitz said.

"Yo," Stanley said.

"Too cloudy if you ask me. No way the Gi-gantes get in nine innings." Coach Kopolwitz sniffed, as if to detect thunderstorms amidst the mushroom gravies.

"We're back from Lucky's. Grapefruits are on special for eighty-nine cents." "I'm not in the market." Stanley Doone liked living in the Blue Horizon. An all-night bodega was on the corner if he wanted bologna. A Walgreen's was two blocks up, if he required Advil or Sudafed. Across the street was a school yard, where, if his work was stalled, he could hang and apply the goad of remembering what it was like to be skinny, near-sighted, and easily whacked at dodge ball. Normally, though, working at the Blue Horizon was cool. His co-habitants' ages and infirmities kept it quiet, private, suited for his labors. Being surrounded by these fragile, unfulfilled folks, slipping steadily from life, fueled his desire to catalog its waste. Once, he had met Mrs. Kopolwitz in the foyer, fumbling in her purse to pay some postage due. She could not find the proper change. She could not grasp it if she did. "It is very hard, dear," she had said, "to wake up every morning, knowing you will see a little worse, hear a little less, ache a little more, watch your friends deteriorate, find another gone." He intended to devote a one-pager to Mrs. Kopolwitz in *Lunacies and Failures*, but he did not want to talk to her now. "I have a date for lunch." "How nice, dear. You ought to be out of your room more."

"Get back, we'll play some one-on-one," Coach Kopolwitz said. "You look like a fellow who can stick the jay." "Sounds good, man."

"Company is tonic for the soul. I've often thought to encourage ..." Mrs. Kopolwitz dropped her voice and pointed at Mr. Rabie's door. "... some of our neighbors to join clubs, become involved with issues, adopt puppies from the SPCA."

"My date digs my ideas."

"Bring her around," Coach Kopolwitz said. "I have ideas she can fool with." "Morris's and my first date was for breakfast. We met at a pep rally before the St. Flannery game." "Betty Coed, here, ordered one English muffin. A woman like that, I figured, knew how to keep her shape." "Morris came to the rally with two friends. They took turns dancing with me." "Nate Weinstein had the car. Frankie Kaye had seventy-five cents to get us inside. I went first to scout the talent." "Nate asked me for a date for the next Saturday. Frankie for the Friday before. This one, Mr. Fast Operator, didn't say a word." "But nine o'clock, next morning, who was knocking on her door?" Coach Kopolwitz took his wife's right hand with his left. Still holding their wagons, they circled Stanley Doone. "Those fellows weren't such Jack Armstrongs I could trust them with my future bride." "When I came home, I told my mother I have met my husband, He is near-sighted, bald and smokes awful cigars." "On your first date? You knew? That happens?"

"We knew." Mrs. Kopolwitz sighed. "It happens. You look very nice, dear. Have a lovely time." Stanley Doone planted his right foot beneath the front wheels of Mrs. Kopolwitz's wagon. He hoisted his left to swing it clear of the Coach's. He felt like some gawky fucking heron about to wade some forbidding fucking swamp.

§

"I had the weirdest dream." Tisa Rio lay on the leather couch. Her purple suede mini-skirt rested above her knees. She was glad she had saved the dream because she was having a bad hour. She was avoiding too many things. How she and Princeton were getting along. How she spent the last part of her morning. Her new ideas about Stanley Doone. She did not want to speak about these things until they were more settled inside her. Until she had control.

Her new thoughts about Stanley Doone were weird. At the same time she could not believe she was having them, she could not wait to see how they connected. It felt like the time Sister Evangeline tipped over a log during a nature walk, uncovered all these squiggley-squirmies, and explained our Lord would not have put them on His earth without a purpose. Still, her dream was a good reason not to talk about her thoughts. Dr. Chumus liked dreams. He beamed like he was getting the most fabulous present in the world. She had rehearsed the dream in the car mirror. She could tell it hellaciously. Dr. Chumus opened his notebook.

"I was, like, gee, back in Sulfleur Pond with Angel Mogilia and Danny Donovan. The first couple in my crowd to get married? Wow! I haven't seen them in years."

"Hmmm."

"It was, like, in this dream, we would get together every morning after breakfast. You know, sit around the table, chat, like neighbors do before the dishes. Like this Lucy-Ethel kind of thing."

"Go on."

"There were, like, troubles in their marriage? And they were moving to Miami, so Danny could get medicine?" She loved it when Dr. Chumus said, "Go on." It was so meaningful. He said "Go on" like it did not matter, but it had to matter because most of the time he said nothing. He sounded totally masterful when he said "Go on." Totally insightful and encouraging. She liked "Go on" more than "How does that make you feel?" or "What are you thinking?" because "How does that make you feel?" or "What are you thinking?" meant she had to talk about "feelings" or "thinkings"; but "Go on" meant anything she said was good enough. "And I said they shouldn't over-rely on this medicine to solve their problems, so long as Angel was still bashing mice. 'Bashing mice.' Those were my exact words."

Usually, Tisa Rio stared at a blank spot on the ceiling. She peeked, now, at Dr. Chumus. Nothing in his manner suggested she was depraved. He wore his denim work shirt and Chi pants. His curly head was bent over his notebook. His fingers scribbled notes to himself. In the Escher print behind him, a flock of white birds, flying left-to-right, turned into a flock of black birds, flying right-to-left. She used to try to identify the point at which the white birds changed into black birds, so she could stop that switch from happening. One day she realized that there was no point. All the black birds and all the white birds were at all times within the frame. If you did not have the black birds, the white birds would be gone. "So we are sitting at this table in this kitchen, and ... And I say this *thing* about 'mice-bashing.' And the dream zooms in tight for, like, this close-up? And Angel's, like, pinching this furry little mouse between her thumb and index finger."

"Hmmm."

"And all the time we're talking, she's, like, smashing its little head on the table. And all the time she's smashing the mouse, the mouse is biting her." BANG! BANG! BANG! Tisa Rio chopped her hand on the leather couch to show how Angel Mogilia was smashing the mouse against the kitchen table. "It was totally disgusting."

Dr. Chumus kept scribbling.

Tisa Rio stretched so she could see her watch. The black birds turned to white and back to black again. You don't have to solve the mysteries of life, she reminded herself. Just live it. She was almost out of there. She was okay with that.

"Bashing mice," Dr. Chumus said.

"Exactly."

"Bashing mice. Bashing mice. Mice bashing. Masturbating. How's your love life, Tisa?" "Whoops," Tisa Rio said.

§

Tisa had asked him to meet at her doctor's office. Stanley Doone arrived twenty minutes early. She had not said what type doctor, and he had expected the usual medical building: crappy design; crappy execution; doctors in cubicles, stacked one upon another like Legos. Instead, he found himself on a cobblestone path, winding through an overgrown garden, toward a gold-and-purple trimmed Victorian. Ivy shoots twisted around his ankles. Blackberry thorns plucked at his sleeves. The garden reminded him of jungles in his comic books, where bitches like Sheena or Nyoka, having already survived crocodiles and wart hogs, would be staked, half-naked, in the center of some fucking tribal compound. He jerked free his legs and arms.

The waiting room was basement level. It was small and low-ceilinged. The smell of earth pressed in from all sides. Stanley Doone sat on an orange shell chair, beside a bamboo table with copies of *The Sun* and *Psychology Today*. It was like being entombed with fucking *Psychology Today*. He did not notice the man in the matching orange chair.

"I never saw you before at Doctor Chester's," the man said.

"I'm not a patient, dude. I'm meeting a friend."

"I am not a patient either. Doctor Chester knows nothing's wrong with me. He refills my S.S.I." Stanley Doone picked up *The Sun*. The "Salute to Erotica" issue.

"Dr. Chester says, 'How are you feeling?' I tell him, 'No change.'" The man lit a half-smoked joint he had been holding beneath his chair. He was a big man with a scarred nose and a rainbow cap. He offered the joint to Stanley Doone, who shook his head. "It does not take five minutes. I keep my check, and he bills them for a full hour. It's nothing sacred and professional, if you know what I mean."

"That's cool."

"If I needed a doctor, Dr. Chester would be fine. You should consider him." "I don't need a doctor, man." Stanley Doone wondered if Tisa knew that her doctor allowed drugs on the premises. That he was down with this fraud. "And I'm not on S.S.I." He wished he had not said that. The man's smile clenched into a scowl. The scowl hardened to stone. He glared as if Stanley Doone was an insect he would slam it on.

A door opened and Tisa Rio came out. A short, bearded man, who might have stepped out of a cartoon by Edward Koren, stood in the corridor behind her. "Oh, hi, Stanley. You found it."

"It wasn't hard." He walked toward her.

"I'm glad you found it."

"I'm glad too."

"'I'm glad,'" said the man in the rainbow cap. "'No, I'm glad.' 'No, I'm glad' 'No, I'm glad too.'" "Mind your own business," Tisa Rio said.

“Fuck you.”

“I’ll be with you in a minute, Jerome,” the bearded man said.

“Fuck you, whore.”

“Jerome, what have we said about sublimating hostilities?” “Whore of Babylon! Whore of Sodom! Whore of Whores!” “Hey, Jerome,” Stanley Doone said. “Put a fucking sock in it, man.” “So now you’re smart. So now you know my name.” Jerome Heavens passed as close to Stanley Doone as he could. “Looks like Mr. Boy Friend’s got a caterpillar on his chin. Watch out somebody don’t mash it.”

PART

THREE.

Three weeks later ...

Chapter XI.

Tisa Rio drove the black Porsche up Sir Francis Drake. She wore a wide-brimmed straw hat, leopard-skin print Capri pants, pink linen shirt from J. Crew, its tail knotted in front so two inches of her tanned tummy showed. She had selected her outfit for the surprise she had in mind. Stanley Doone looked like he had gotten enough into the spirit to find a t-shirt and khakis he had not used to dry the dog.

"Where're we going?" Stanley Doone said.

"Picnic."

"*Pic*-nic?"

Tisa Rio had been seeing Stanley Doone two or three times a week. The days she did not see him, she spoke to him on the phone. She spoke to him on the phone on days she saw him too. Sometimes she spoke to him two or three times. If he did not call her, she would call him, and they would talk about what they had done that day or the day before or what they would do tomorrow. She and he walked in North Beach or Chinatown. They walked in Golden Gate Park or took the ferry to Sausalito. They sipped espresso at sidewalk cafes and laughed at people passing by.

Stanley Doone no longer dropped in on Princeton Gutkin. He did call to make sure his case was being pursued. Princeton assured him it was. He was tracking down a key witness. When Stanley asked how a witness had been discovered this late in the process, Princeton said the man was not exactly a witness. But he could tie up the case's loose ends. He laughed when he said this. He said the man was difficult to locate because he lived in a van.

"I've never been on a real picnic," Stanley Doone said. "An archetypal Norman-fucking Rockwell picnic, man. A picnic that was fun."

"All my picnics are fun."

They had left Sir Francis Drake and were climbing a two-lane road lined by eucalyptus. Stanley Doone considered the new feelings he had been having as if he had lifted them in tweezers from a petri dish. Before he had begun seeing Tisa, the strips of bark peeling from the tree trunks would have reminded him of flagellations. Now there was a creek beside the road that might have been "babbling." A deer beside the creek could have been Bambi. He did not believe in the Divine, but his perceptions' change seemed more dazzling than any Burning Bush. He had never experienced "Love," but he had caught himself humming tunes that could only have been composed with his new feelings in mind. "I've never been on a picnic where my father didn't wallop me for forgetting the mustard, or my mother's potato salad hadn't spoiled, or I didn't fucking chase a ball into poison sumac."

"Today, you are with me. And I give good picnic."

"In college, on a field trip to sketch landscapes, I was on a picnic that seemed to have the whole trip going. Green grass, man. Warm sun. The crust trimmed off the fucking sandwiches. Then the wind shifted ..." Stanley Doone wrinkled his nose. "You ever smell week-old dead cow?"

"*Stan*-ley!"

Tisa Rio parked on the south face of Mt. Tam.

"Need help?" Stanley Doone said.

"No. This is on me."

Tisa Rio carried the wicker basket in her right hand, the blanket in her left. Stanley Doone followed her up a narrow path through a redwood grove. Fallen leaves padded the ground. The air was moist and cool. Shafts of sunlight fell between the branches.

"I could carry something," Stanley Doone said.

"I work out every day. You never pump anything heavier than a pen. I could put you on your back in thirty seconds." "I can handle hard labor, man. I'm no total feeb. I get over my injuries, I'll show you." "Don't get over anything until Princeton hands you a check. That's a major investment your feeb-ness is protecting. The insurance company could have somebody with a camera shooting pictures of you now." "They don't they believe I'm hurt?"

"That's how the game is played."

"I resent the accusation, man. That is no way fair. My condition's documented by unanimous medical opinion." Stanley Doone pushed his glasses up his nose. But was it fair for him to hide how he had practically caused his injury? For him to see Tisa without telling Princeton? He had shown himself as someone who, when opportunity arose, knew how to take advantage. He dug, in fact, his new found, ruthless edge. The insurance company had the right idea. He deserved surveillance.

The trail had left the grove. It climbed through dusty scrub. It switched back every twenty, thirty, forty yards. The ground was dry and skittery. Stanley Doone limped and groaned.

"Are you all right?"

"In case the tricky bastards have got sound."

Tisa Rio leaned into the hill. She fixed her eyes a few feet in front of her lead boot. She visualized her thighs pumping like pistons that would drive her to the top. She repeated silently: "The seeker stumbles. But she need not fall." The morning had sucked. Her mother had called in the middle of her pelvic tilts. Dad's kidney was shot. Eddie, Jr. and Faye had the kids at Bubble Beach. Aunt Rhoda and Uncle Gideon spent a week in Boca. Freddy Drummer had scored a plaque for twenty-five years with the school district. Each time her mother revealed another twenty-five year plaque, Tisa felt someone twist her bi-cuspid with pliers. Every "Remember little Tiffany Tupperware? She's married with twins" felt like another staple punched into her tongue. The steady diet of the whatevers that her mother set before her was as yummy as charcoal briquets on brown rice. Each cheesy, hum-drum inanity, whether hoisted into the chatter with a trumpet flourish or slipped in casually, like a *Watchtower* beneath the door — slapped her as a trashing of her own adventurous ways.

And Princeton was doing nothing to restore her self-esteem She would have thought he would have appreciated her doing him this favor, but he acted like lunch with Stanley Doone was normal behavior. Like Stanley was too booked with airline stewardesses and dental technicians to register her concession. Instead of being grateful and attentive, Princeton buried deeper into his research and investigations.

Stanley was grateful and attentive. He was considerate of her feelings. Half the time she did not even think of the money he would be getting. She had stopped telling Princeton whom she was seeing. Why should she, if he didn't care? If she was not home, let him think she was massaging extra clients. It was not like she had anything to hide. It was not like she and Stanley were, for God's sake, doing anything. He was a perfect gentleman. It was weird, he was such a gentleman.

Sometimes, though, she thought about the money. She could not help herself. It did not mean she was a materialistic person, but it had to be, at least, a million dollars. Princeton had never worked so hard. He had never had a million dollar case, and she bet this was it. She had seen a million dollars once — one-hundred ten-thousand dollar bills in the lobby of Bally's boardwalk casino, frozen behind glass, trimmed by a chorus line of flashing light bulbs, guarded by blue uniformed men the height and width of grizzly bears. She saw a million dollars on Princeton's desk. Pritikin was dealing one ten-thousand dollar bill to Princeton and two to Stanley; and she was snapping her head back and forth like fans at Wimbledon.

Two-thirds of a million was serious money. She wondered how Stanley would react if someone told him he could score more. If he told Princeton he would not settle unless Princeton cut his fee to twenty-five or twenty or, even, ten percent, she bet Princeton would do it. He would curse and threaten, but he would. Ten percent of a million dollars was more than he could make on half his other cases combined. He would do it if he needed the money, and she could convince him he did. He would do it if he believed Stanley was serious, and she could help there too. "He is such an individual person," she heard herself say. "He never had money, and he lives like he doesn't need any. I bet he means it, hon."

But if she was going to help Stanley, there had to be something in it for her. She had thought about that too. Just for practice. Just for fun. Like she was making up a plot for some *Murder She Wrote*. So at one of Princeton's cocktail parties, she had asked Sandor Weill, the divorce lawyer, whose money it was if someone who was injured got married. "That is a very complex issue, young lady." He had drawn close, taken her arm, stared at her ta-tas. Sandor Weill was about five-two. He was flanked by two six-foot blondes, who did not speak or move, as if they were props wheeled with him to public appearances. "But as things stand, if a man is injured while wed but separates from his spouse before his case concludes, the funds become his separate property. Conversely, if an injured bachelor obtains a recovery after marrying, the proceeds are half the little woman's as a community asset."

"Wasn't the Backpack Killer around here?" Stanley Doone said.

"I guess so. I don't remember."

"You don't remember?" Stanley Doone had stopped climbing. "Stopped hikers. Asked them for trail mix or goose down. Blew twelve of them away."

"I remember. I just don't think about it."

"Amazing, man. I can't believe you can venture into these fucking wilds without considering the Backpack Killer. I bet when you go to movies you don't pin-point the fire exits first thing. You don't plot the most direct route or calculate the one with the fewest people in the way, adjusting for old women and small children, who can be shoved aside if things get sticky."

Like Princeton said, Tisa Rio thought, Stanley had interesting ideas. But he was always tripping on death. How it was the one great subject. How no one faced it squarely but him. He always tried to get her to talk about death. "What do they do with dead guppies, man?" he would ask, passing a pet store. "Flush them down the toilet? Fertilize the African violets? What about the dead turtles, parakeets, monkeys, dogs?" "Every New York Yankee will die," he would announce, glancing at a softball game. "Every New York Met. Everyone in every phone directory. Everyone who ever knew you or saw you or spoke your name."

One afternoon, crossing Washington Square, he had gripped her arm hard enough to pinch. "I can prove the world is insane, man, if you don't believe me. 'A fundamental mental derangement characterized by lost contact with reality.' That's the meaning of psychosis. So anyone who lives under a set of unreal assumptions is, by definition, fucking mad." Stanley had pointed at the cross on St. Peter and Paul's. "Is Jesus the Son of God? Is Mohammed his prophet? Does Moses or Buddha or Confucius speak his word? If there is one God, which is the number I keep hearing, only one of them can have it right. So everyone who bases their life on another guys' teachings is acting under a delusion. And if there is no God, or several, or one, but none of the cats mentioned, all their followers are fucking bonkers." Stanley had relaxed his grip. "It's the fear of death that drives them off the edge. That makes them hallucinate these folks to hide behind."

Tisa Rio had not been thrilled at Stanley declaiming so close to St. Peter and Paul's. It would have been okay with her if he had held off until they were around the corner. It was not like she had a smidgen of her old beliefs, but why ask for trouble? Stanley acted like thinking about death made him brave and masterful, but Tisa thought he had these ideas because he was scared too. He reminded her of when she was five or six and would snuggle against her mother and ask if witches and dragons were real. "No," her mother would say, "Witches and dragons aren't real." Then she would ask if burglars and robbers were real, hoping her mother would deny their existence too. "Not around here," was all her mother would say. Tisa was not sure what to say to Stanley Doone.

"They never caught the Backpack Killer, you know. My theory is he's been quiet so long because the Zebra Killer or the Zodiac Killer or some other Killer got him. That would be cool. One horror eliminating another. Otherwise, he could be out here. We could cross a creek and be blown away. He could be you, for all I know. For all you know, he's me. It's terrifying, man, if you think about it."

"'If,' Stanley, that's the key. You can't spend your whole life worrying. You could walk out your front door and get hit by a truck."

"Yo. Try not to remind me."

When they were in the sun, Tisa Rio spread the blanket. She lay out the pate and cheese, the fruit and sourdough baguettes, the red wine and nut brownies. Below lay soft hills, green tree-top beds, a stretch of turquoise bay, cut like a red-orange sash by the Golden Gate Bridge.

"Far fucking-out," Stanley Doone said.

"It was supposed to be gold. But the primer looked so fine, public opinion made them leave it." "You're kidding?"

Tisa shrugged. When she had lived in Sulfleur Pond Stanley was the last guy her dreams would have set beside her on a mountain. But they would not have booked her into Princeton's penthouse either. Dreams, it turned out, were not a perfect navigational system. She had not dreamed, to be real, about third eyes or ten thousand dollar bills either. Yet they bubbled inside her now, sometimes one riding on top, sometimes the other. The transitoriness of which ruled implied the mix had room for more. She wondered what the next boil would bring. She was damned if it would be the same as what had settled over her folks and Eddie, Jr. like a chloroform-soaked shroud.

"I'd like to know if that was true." Stanley Doone tore off a hunk of baguette. He felt that, since Tisa had talked about the bridge, he should talk about something. He could think of nothing to say. "I'm working on this new story. Four pages, maybe six. About this chick let her eleven-month-old starve."

"Stanley! That is so dumb!"

"She had her first kid at thirteen. Then she had six more. The psychologists said she was not vengeful, man, or vindictive. She just did not know how to tell if her kids were sick or healthy, if they had fever or were growing normally. When her son was dying, man, of pneumonia and starvation, she thought he was a skinny baby with a head cold."

"That is gross. You are totally depressing."

Stanley Doone looked at the bridge. "The ozone layer's fucked. AIDS and crack have wiped out half a generation. A guy who co-starred in flicks with a chimp, a rube with the I.Q. of an eggplant and the social conscience of a staph infection's twice elected president, and I'm depressing. Whoa!"

"Well, starving babies, Stanley. Imagine thinking things like that all day. What's a person supposed to say? You should learn personal enjoyment."

"I enjoy myself. I laugh every time I hear these calls to fucking return to fucking family values, man. As if it wasn't fucking families who produced the fucking people who established the fucking society that turned out the fucking citizens whose fucking behavior created the fucking situations the fucking callers for 'return' fucking object to. Man, I fucking chuckle when I see God is just one more uninformed mother, putting children on earth with no clue what they need. He is not cruel, just stupid."

Tisa Rio took his hand. "When you settle your case, you'll have lots of money. You'll be able to do lots of really nice things. Has Princeton told you how much you will get?"

"Not exactly."

"It will be a lot. Won't that be nice?"

Stanley Doone nodded.

"Won't it be nice to be able to afford whatever you want, for whomever you want it?" Tisa Rio placed Stanley Doone's hand on her breast. One of things he did not do was take it away. "My doctor tells me, 'From every desire's seed forests may come.'" She kissed him. "Awesome, Stanley. Have you been practicing?"

Stanley Doone could not believe that had happened. He wanted to kiss Tisa again. He could not believe no one was around to stop him. The wind had shifted. He crinkled his nose.

"Goddamn you." Tisa jumped on him, laughing.

"Sorry." Stanley Doone had fallen backwards. Tisa was on top, a knee on each arm, pinning him to the ground the way Willie Ott, in elementary school, had pinned him during recess. Pinned him and pinched his cheeks and tossed his glasses into the ivy. Willie, the tough guy. Willie, the admired. Willie, who had drowned. Stanley wondered how Tisa had learned this predatory move. Above them, hung a hawk, hunting on the breeze. "I couldn't help it. You reminded me."

"*Me*. Of dead cows." She was fumbling with his fly.

"Tisa!"

"*Stan*-ley !"

Her hand was on it.

"Friendly little fellow. I think he wants to play. Hmmm, he's not so little after all. Good thing that truck didn't hit you there. It could've cracked an axle."

“Forest rangers might be around.”

“Then hush. You’ll roust Smokey the Bear.”

Tisa was doing things unmentioned in the songs he hummed. Stanley Doone felt his body accommodate itself to her as if it had been subscribing to X-rated adult ed courses without his knowledge.

When they had finished, Tisa rolled to one side. “That was very *nice*, Stanley . That was better than nice. You could have a future in this work.” Stanley Doone drew his fingers through the dirt. “In some societies, this would mean we’re engaged.” “Do not shit a shitter,” Tisa Rio said.

Chapter XII.

"I thought I had no case."

"I may have been hasty in my conclusion."

"'Hasty.' While the whistle in my heart is killing me."

The wine on the table was burgundy. The steaks were rare. The red velvet wallpaper tinted even the water pink. Princeton Gutkin cut his line of thinking short of spurting-jugular associations. "Refill?"

His guest covered his glass.

"Peach melba? Chocolate mousse?"

"'*Hasty*.'" If the first enunciation of the word had scrubbed it in lye, this repetition toweled it with barbed wire.

No maniacal cackle rocked his resurrected client. No unhinged gibbering flecked saliva on his chin.. Indeed, Jerome Heavens sat as ordinary as a 38 Geary bus. But Morgan Beaujack had not misspoken. The freakshow was as wrapped in his obsession as tightly as a Blue Point oyster its shell. That did not mean, however, he retained the same game plan for alleviating his situation. It was not certain he would buy the modification Gutkin had in mind. "About this surgeon ..."

"YOU KNOW HIM?"

"I ..."

"WHERE IS HE?"

The blue haired woman at the next table dropped her bread stick. The conventioneers in town from St. Paul burrowed deeper into their assessment of Pier 39. The waiter became drawn to a soup spoon that required buffing. And the maitre d' appeared to seek his next line in a teleprompter in the ceiling. "His receptionist says the doctor has left town. But I know the receptionist is lying. Everyone I ask is lying. Every day, I hear the doctor laugh. Every day, I smell the doctor's breath. I feel him tap the keys that keep me screwed up good." Jerome Heavens whirled as if expecting to find Esubiuo Chabchap, M.D., brussels sprouts behind his ear, celery stalk in his lapel, camouflaged amidst the salad bar. "You know where he is, you tell me."

"I've never met the gentleman," Princeton Gutkin said. "But your story's sincerity touched me. So I checked it out." Jerome Heavens waited.

Princeton Gutkin waited too. Until this point, he had regarded himself as, fundamentally, a man of law and his transgressions as mere redistributions of a few dimes out of all the world's dollars. With money known to be evil's root — the fabled buyer of no happiness — what did it matter how some settlement disbursals broke? Besides, the codifiers and enforcers of the standards which condemned his filchings had attained prominence only because they had stolen greater sums than he. Or because they were the sons of men who had. Or sons of sons of sons. One benefit of life in late twentieth century America was that all the myths were slain. Everybody knew those John Wayne-inspiring pioneers had slaughtered Indians, robbed Mexicans, and enslaved Africans to reduce start-up costs in launching the good old U.S.A. Then, to boost their holdings, they had torched its forests, poisoned its rivers, broke its women and children in their mines and mills.

Given that understanding, Princeton Gutkin was uncertain why his link to law remained important. Why he had not previously recognized it as one more vestigial moral appendix — another useless wall. Nicholas Phillipoulos had handed him a key. But Gutkin feared that if he turned it — swung the handle — stepped across the threshold — he would leave the repairable relativity of sums for a universally condemned absolute, where no restitution could be made, which would mark him as a man of law no more.

But Gutkin moved. For in the moment that he hesitated, nothing shook the red-rich room sufficiently to alter his life situation. If God wants His Commandments obeyed, he thought, hey, LET GOD SHOW IT. Morality was one thing — and that thing was cold, abstract, unreal. Tisa was something else — alive and warm and requiring spring wardrobes. His ledger was real too — visible and vocal and standing short in the comfort column. Most important was HIS REALITY. He had labored to build the monument that was his self. The effort he had put into its construction matched that of any schmuck slave-labor gang hauling rocks up some farshimelt pharaoh's tomb. He believed the present he had achieved from his past equivalent to some mythological beast coalesced from of the rumors and half-sightings reported by several centuries' tongues. He was Princeton Gutkin — GRAND, UNIQUE, FABULOUS. And here came douche-bag Stanley Doone, threatening to cut off his balls and feed him to the Bar Association.

"My operative's report is in," he said, "With disturbing findings." "Damn right, 'disturbing.' My nipples feel chewed by wolverines." "Forget about your self a second."

"Huh?"

"Don't be so frigging self-absorbed — excuse my French — when national security may be in issue." Jerome Heavens lifted a serrated knife.

"Your Dr. Chabchap is only the tip of the iceberg. One piece in the jigsaw puzzle." "'Iceberg?' 'Jigsaw?'" Jerome Heavens chopped his knife up and down, dicing nothing into nothing else.

Princeton Gutkin had not expected his tablemate to welcome metaphor. But, he thought, to hit the 10.0, you must step from the high board for the matchbook pool. For both ears and the tail, you leaned into the horns to plant the blade. "You would not believe the shit his network's into. It's kicked hell out of innocents for years. Mothers. Children. Cripples. Nuns. It's the gold standard for fucking people up. But Chabchap's just a stooge. My investigator's I.D.'d the man on top. If you're up to it, maybe, we can even scores."

The blue-haired woman had disappeared into the smoke from the mesquite grill. The conventioneers had abandoned their quail-ka-bob and Coho salmon. The waiter and maitre conferred beside the dessert cart. Princeton Gutkin wondered if he had gone too far. Maybe, he should have omitted "Nuns." But Jerome Heavens nodded, no more surprised at the existence of conspiracy than an assertion your johnson smarted if stropped on a cross-cut saw.

Princeton Gutkin took a photograph from his wallet. "Burn this, when you have committed it to memory." "This is him?"

"A real bad-ass. If only something could be done."

"You can tell. Something in the eyes. Makes you want to put a bullet there" "Time is of the essence. More people suffer every day."

Jerome Heavens drummed his knife's point on the photograph of Stanley Doone. "You know, I've seen this guy around."

CREAM TEAM

Chapter XIII.

Tisa Rio waited for the customer with the vented sharkskin moccasins to come out of the dressing room. She wore lavender satin short-shorts and a lavender satin basketball shirt with the number 36-22-36 outlined in sequins on her back. All Francisco Femmes' girls wore the same uniform. "The Cream Team," management advertised them.

It had been two weeks since she had balled Stanley Doone. Hell, practically raped him. Stanley acted like they were married already. Opened doors. Carried packages. It was sort of cute. She bought him little presents now — a crystal tear drop, a milk chocolate heart — waiting for his settlement so he could buy big ones for her.

Morgan Beaujack had a Turkish towel knotted on his hip. He thought he had picked a good one. He liked that honey blonde hair. He liked those biceps and quads. And that sneer. He loved that goddamn sneer.

"Now this is your massage. Tell me what you like."

"Anything you got, foxy lady, is okay with me." Morgan Beaujack lay, stomach down, on the table's heated sheet.

"We don't need barriers," Tisa Rio said, unknotting the towel, "if we're going to be friends." "Friends is definitely how to go."

"It's not like I'm going to hurt you."

Morgan Beaujack let her pull away the towel. The air smelled of strawberry incense. The tape deck played an all-strings "Stairway to Heaven." The paintings swirled Day-Glo oranges and purples like they came from Timothy Leary's garage sale.

"Where would you like me to start?"

"How's the legs sound? Then shoulders and back."

"Awesome. Working towards the center heightens awareness. Saves the best for last." Tisa Rio rubbed the oil into Morgan Beaujack's thighs. "You want anything special, ask."

"I like the way you think, Monique. That's your name, right, 'Monique'?"

"That's right. Monique, Dr. Kissinger."

"Monique's a nice name." Morgan Beaujack closed his eyes. This one was not bad. She even knew something about massage. He imagined the ripplings of the muscles in her arms as her fingers brought him through pleasure to the brink of pain and safely back again. She was not one of those butch man-haters, digging their nails into your lats until you screamed, then chirping, innocent, about nasty tensions trapped inside you. This Monique was smooth.

So what if he had tension? Who had a better right to tension than him? He had Amethyst. He had his suspension. He had some goddamn nut leaving the same goddamn message on his goddamn Codaphone sixteen goddamn times a day. "I know who you are. I know what you did. You will pay and pay." That voice was goddamn spooky. He near jumped every time he saw the red light on. And when he needed stress reduction more than ever, goddamn Inge had to get herself deported over that hanky-panky with that Roumanian string quartet, that airedale, and those handcuffs. It was such a hassle finding proper help these days.

"It's such a hassle these days, Monique. You know what I'm saying? 'S a jungle out there." "Hassles? Tell me about it." Tisa Rio massaged the sole of Morgan Beaujack's foot with the heel of her hand. "I sure do. Believe me." "'Be a professional.' That's what my parents said. 'So whatever happens, you can make a living.' 'Living,' hah! The future of medicine in this country, Monique, is in the goddamn toilet. Goddamn H.M.O.s springing up everywhere. Goddamn docs-in-the-box, franchised like McDonalds. Goddamn managed care, stuffing us into bins, turning us into one more goddamn commodity for shoppers to paw over. My parents should only have been sharp enough to have foreseen free agency. They should have slapped me every time I reached for *Basic Chemistry* and sent me to the schoolyard to learn to hit the curve. Any asshole utility infielder's making multiples more than me." Morgan Beaujack let both arms hang over the table and shook his wrists. "Now, you guys, you got yourself a nice thing going. You come in, your customers're lined up, waiting. You do your job, get paid, go home. You got no costs, no decisions, no payroll. All the time, nice music's playing." "You know, us girls've got problems too. It's not like everything we make is gravy. Like, you pay thirty-five dollars for a massage, right? Management gets half of that. And for sure, we get tips — fifty dollars, a hundred, say Two hundred if we do something really special. But management makes sure it gets its share. Management fines you fifty dollars for leaving on a light, a hundred for being late, two-fifty for letting in police without a warrant." Tisa Rio rotated Morgan Beaujack's right arm. "The end of each month, management charges each girl a hundred fifty for attorney fees. I asked my boyfriend — he's a lawyer — if that was legal. He laughed. 'What a great idea. Every employer in California ought to be required to charge every employee one hundred fifty dollars a month for attorney fees. The Bar could hold it in trust and, the end of the year, divvy it up among us.' Then, soon as the customers get tired of you, management lets you go. No retirement, no health plan, no nothing." "That don't sound fair. You gals ought to protest. Make one hell of a picket line for 'Eyewitness News' to cover." "Uh-uh. You don't protest to management. That fat guy on the stool on your way in?" "Five-ten, 300 pounds, wearing a cowboy hat and Tony Lama boots?" "That's management. That's Billy Fu. Billy lives in Piedmont and drives a Silver Cloud. I mean, his chauffeur drives. Billy drinks banana daiquiris in back and watches MTV. According to his probation, Billy can't own massage parlors, so this one's in his ex-wife's name. I've never seen her in my life; but Billy's here every day, sitting on that stool, singing 'You Need Hands to Show Someone You Love Them,' grab-assing the girls. Only one kind of employee relations Billy's got in mind." "I see what you mean. No matter what line of work you're in, the goddamn power structure rigs it so you can't get ahead. Take this chest cutter I knew from Merritt-Peralta. Guy's been doing business with this company makes pace-makers. Only the company's got cash flow problems, due to rising costs of production versus limited market demand. They hire him to goose interest along. By prescribing pace-makers for fifty, sixty patients don't quite need one. Besides the normal surgeon's fee, the guy negotiates himself five figures down, a ten percent kickback, plus, get this, stock options." "Gee." Tisa Rio rubbed in more oil. "Billy Fu'd never give us stock options." "Probably left the poor bastard lots of time to provide quality care to the underprivileged. But anybody think of that? Shit, no." Morgan Beaujack wiggled around on the table. "A little more right there. Lower. Lower. Yeah." "He got in trouble? Your friend?"

"They threw his ass in jail. You tell me why? Anybody's gonna need a good pace maker, right? German engineering. Jap design. Runs like a goddamn clock. Leaves you ten times better off than that misfiring, untuned, clogged-up piece of crap you had before. Just giving natural processes a hand. Goddamn new set of plumbing is all. Do more for you than the goddamn gas station sells you new radials when you still got plenty tread. Than the goddamn bought-and-sold politicians gift-wrapping federal subsidies to the Russian dressing lobby. Nobody slams the gas station owner in jail. Nobody smears him all over the newspapers so his family's goddamn breakfast gets spoiled."

§

The Seville was parked in a yellow zone on Leavenworth. The moon was the green of cataracts. The air smelled of gasoline. Morgan Beaujack breathed deeply, threw his shoulders back, and smiled. That Monique had been inhibited at first. But when he promised her two bills, she had laid that strap on enough to make him glow. He had not believed anybody tipped her two hundred dollars before. He had figured she had said that hoping to score fifty or a hundred. But he had promised two bills to see how she would go. She had gone fine. She had earned every goddamn penny. He had stoked the glow with two lines in the dressing room. Now he was goddamn burning. The wind tossed crumpled newspaper around like confetti.

"For my first trick ..." The bum wore a grenadier's coat: blue wool; red epaulets; gold buttons. Busted veins had swollen his nose purple. He plucked a paper cup from a trash basket.

Morgan Beaujack stopped. Your garden variety street crazy slunk by, gaze fixed on invisible demons, or stormed past, cursing Hebrew bankers.

He felt good enough to give this one a chance to make a buck.

The crazy swung the cup in barrel loops and figure eights.

"All *riiight*!" Morgan Beaujack said. The wind hooted both of them on. The stoplight fired RED — RED — RED.

The crazy crashed the cup through a power dive, then contemplated it like the skull of Yorick.

Morgan Beaujack clapped. No one else was on the street. No cars were moving. Being the entire audience for this mad recital felt eerie. It also felt goddamn exciting.

The crazy grabbed a second cup out of the trash and swung both around, one trailing the other. At first, their flight paths demonstrated disciplined team-work. Then he launched two solo displays.

Maybe, Morgan Beaujack thought, it was a sign. Maybe he had been tapped to witness the birth of the latest, hippest thing. In a culture that had near-landed the inventor of the Pet Rock on the *Fortune* "500," a lunatic with wit and irony could be the future. The right management, the packaging and pub could break this bizzaro nationwide. He imagined his discovery cover-storied in *Esquire* and *GQ* and chatting up Phil Donohue and Oprah. He imagined himself scouring the city's flop houses and back alleys, rounding up an entire performance troupe. From the looks of Napoleon, Jr.'s cost of food and clothing, it could outperform Real Estate Investment Trusts. Too bad he did not have a personal services contract handy.

"For my finale ..." The crazy tossed both cups over his shoulder.

Morgan Beaujack was considering his future as an impresario of the deranged when he turned on his ignition.

"Do not turn around."

Morgan Beaujack glanced at the rearview mirror. It had been ripped from its stem.

"Do not be scared. We will take a ride. Because I have a gun ..." Something hard and cold touched the back of Morgan Beaujack's neck. "... does not mean I will use it."

"Where should I go?"

"I never rode in a Cadillac. I bet your mileage sucks."

"I don't have much money."

"If I wanted money, I would ask?"

Morgan Beaujack thought he knew that voice. It was like the voice on his Codaphone. But it was like some voice before.

"Drive how I tell you. I know where we can talk."

Morgan Beaujack pulled away from the curb. The voice's tone — pleasant, conversational — urged him toward moderation. Everything else made him want to crap his pants. The green moon leered through his side window. The traffic lights struck his eyes like thumbs. I am a physician, he reminded himself. Physicians are not kidnapped in their Cadillacs. This is not Mexico City. This is not goddamn Beirut. He drove in the direction the voice commanded.

Their ride, while meandering, did not seem to Morgan Beaujack more Hell-ridden than any other. The golden arches proclaiming the drek of Chicken McNuggets on near every corner did not mean that madness ruled the land. The purple Mohawked skateboarder's helmetless, pellmell descent of the Hayes Street hill did not guarantee that brains must be splattered across asphalt. The discharge of the Opera House's designer-wardrobed patrons into Civic Center Plaza, where the most ravaged of the city's homeless roosted, did not compel the conclusion that any breastbone would be ripped apart the width of this societal schism. Symbols, shit, were for professors note cards, not his goddamn life. And there were other symbols on wheels or feet or posted before drive-ins, from which other conclusions could be drawn, if he could only dislodge this goddamn, indelible one which clung, as if with rappaling hooks, to his imagination's walls.

A black-and-white sat in front of a diner on the Embarcadero. Morgan Beaujack considered cutting the wheel, flooring the accelerator, charging across the double set of railroad tracks, crashing into the gold star. That thinking, he told himself, was insane. If the man was going to shoot him, he would shoot him when he swerved. If the man was not going to shoot him, he would have broad-sided a patrol car for no reason. He could be killed in the collision. He would ruin his Seville. He would have exposed himself to pain and humiliation for no gain. The man was not going to shoot him. If the man had not shot him in the Tenderloin, why should he shoot him somewhere else? The man wanted something. As long as I am alive, he thought, I can act or talk my way free. The cocaine still had his shoulders kicked back and his spine stiffened. He focused on the thrill of walking along one more spooky edge. The thrill was giving into the power and not quite knowing how it would be applied.

The man was humming a Monk tune: "Little Rootie Toot."

"Stop."

Morgan Beaujack did.

"Shut the lights."

Morgan Beaujack did.

They sat in the Seville in a parking lot behind an abandoned factory. The cyclone fence around the parking lot sagged from its poles. The windows had been smashed. The spray paint on the walls said: WHITE PUNKS ON DOPE; STOP U.S. OPPRESSION; THIS SPACE CAN BE YOURS. The once electrified sign on the roof said KWILTY-Something. The factory was on a spit of land protruding into the Bay. Around them, the wind howled.

"Go forward. Slow."

The Seville pitched across the parking lot. "Must be goddamn good money in macadam," Morgan Beaujack said. "Somebody hauled so much away."

The man did not say anything.

"Hope I don't blow a tire. Be one hell of a spot to call Triple A." The man did not laugh. "We can walk from here."

Morgan Beaujack got out first. He saw a Firebird, its tires gone, its doors and trunk and hood, its seats and instruments and steering column. If he ran one direction, he would snap an ankle in a hole or shred himself on the cyclone fencing. If he ran in another, he would hit the bay with its cold, its currents, its sharks. He could smell the salt of the bay and the fetid mud flats on its rim. He could hear a freighter moan. Overhead, the

Bay Bridge towered, immense and dark and cannonading with its load: twin decks; ten lanes; vehicles racing, full-throttled, east and west. He was pummeled by the wind.

When he was on the bridge, Morgan Beaujack often fantasized its collapse: the shake and snap and buckle; the cars veering and colliding; the squealing brakes and shrieking tires, dropping through the hole. He would see himself in his Seville, in the water, cars and cables and girders crashing around him. He would try to think what he would do, for he knew that could occur. He knew it would occur. That bridge must collapse at some moment. Though he had that fantasy often, he could think of nothing except let the water swallow him.

When the man stepped in front of him, Morgan Beaujack did not recognize the rainbow cap. He did remember the scarred nose. "Someone told Dr. Chabchap 'Hide.'"

Morgan Beaujack tried to speak but the wind blew away his words. He tried to move but his muscles only quivered. Across the bay were the lights of Oakland and Berkeley and Richmond. They were far away. He could not tell if the moan was the freighter's or his own. He remembered a Nina Simone song — a freighter — a black freighter — and pirates slaughtering townsfolk in their beds.

"I expect someone was you."

"No, I ..."

"You should not make me ask you twice."

"Yes, I ..."

"I do not want to hear *that*!" Jerome Heavens yanked Morgan Beaujack around. They faced the factory, its shattered windows like gouged sockets, its blistered paint spread across the walls like cancerous cells.

"You can have my money, credit cards, my Omega watch, my last ounce of coke — it's pharmaceutical grade. You see these moccasins I'm wearing? Five hundred dollars at Wilkes. But

listen to me, please ..."

"Look at that!" Jerome Heavens pointed at the factory.

"Yes, oh, what ..."

"Right there."

Morgan Beaujack looked around. There was no hope. There was no help. He had said it all. He had offered everything. There was the green moon and the black, fetid bay and the ripping, slicing wind. It had come to this. He did not know where the mistake had been made. He was unsure, if he could go back in time, to where he should return or which action correct to avoid this judgment. He would re-do anything that might be required. He swore this commitment. He awaited intervention — a raising — transport to somewhere far away and glorious. His nose was running and he wiped it on his sleeve.

"I did not want that doctor cutting."

"Yes, no, why ..."

"I wanted no such thing."

"Uh-huh, huh, huh ..."

"I knew about doctors. I told the company about my mother, but they knew better than me. 'Go to this doctor, Jerome.' 'Go to that doctor, Jerome.' 'You want your job, Jerome, you see the doctor.' I told them, but you think they listened. All they listened to was themselves saying 'Doctor,' like 'Doctor' was the end. I thought, Okay, maybe I am wrong. I am willing to consider. They told me 'See the doctor,' and the doctor did to me."

Morgan Beaujack was crying too loudly to hear.

"You work for companies, you break your back. You work at ball, you bust your knees. You work in offices, you strangle your heart. You do not work and you will starve. You have to live, and life will kill you. The company hurt me and the company is gone. The doctor hurt me and the doctor is gone. As Father Dynamite instructed. 'The way of all things.'"

Jerome Heavens' howl melded with the voices of the freighter and the wind, swung across the universe, embraced his dancing mother, linked the Big Bang's beat to his Walther's fire.

Chapter XIV.

"Is there another Morgan Beaujack in San Francisco?" Tisa Rio said. "Doctor? Forty-nine?" Princeton Gutkin grunted.

"Didn't he work up cases for you? Didn't you know him pretty good?" Her words were coming quicker. The coffee cup in her hand was shaking. She had been acting screwy the last couple weeks, Princeton Gutkin thought. Now she looked like she was about to lose it all over her Granola. "The hell you talking about?" Tisa Rio pushed the *Chronicle* across the breakfast table.

"Jesus Christ."

"This city is sick, sick, sick," Tisa Rio said. "I told you we ought to get away." "Soon." Even reading the story, seeing the words turn into pictures, feeling the pictures claw into his nerves, Princeton Gutkin felt he could manage. He could lift his coffee and drink. He could bite his toast. He could make himself say "Soon." "'Soon,'" Tisa Rio said.

"The Doone case is getting ready to resolve. Then we can have that vacation." "Oh?" Tisa Rio emptied her cup in the sink. "I didn't know you were that close. How close? You have any idea?" "A couple days. A couple weeks. Soon."

"I bet Mr. Doone will be happy. Have you told him the good news?" "Nah." Princeton Gutkin stared at the article. "Nothing's final. No sense him counting chickens." "Do you ..." Tisa Rio squirted pink soap onto the sponge and began washing her cup. "... have any idea how much he'll be getting?" "Plenty. The guy'll make a real killing." Princeton Gutkin's laugh came out like a snarl. He remembered the story from high school about the baby blue '55 T-bird, with under a thousand miles, on sale for a hundred dollars. The story was the T-bird had been found in the Lagunitas woods with a body in the trunk that had been there three years, and no one could get out the smell. The story was a gag. He wondered what a Seville would cost with a body there one week. "Morgan was into weird shit. Anybody could have done that to him." "Anybody could have shot him in both eyes?"

Tisa Rio sounded calm but she was wiping the same cup. Wiping and wiping and wiping. "That makes me feel loads better. Swell."

§

Jerome Heavens took one dribble from the foul line and jammed.

He was on the north court at the school yard, across the street from the Blue Horizon. The sky was darkening. The ocean wind tore shreds from the fog and flung them against walls. His head was warm inside his rainbow cap. His ankles were tight inside his black-and-red Air Jordans. They ran three-on-three on the south court. Another half-dozen fools sat on the bench, smoking weed, drinking Stroh's, waiting winners. A shaggy golden retriever lay on the ground, its head between its paws, a yellow tennis ball in front of its nose.

It was crunch time. There were ten seconds to go, and he was down one. He had the ball; and he was backing in, juking and head-faking and double-pumping. The whole team was trying to stop him; and there was no referee, and there were no rules. The whole team hammered his arms and chopped his legs. He used his elbows for a lever, a shoulder for a wedge. He fought clear for his moment of explosion. It was the perfect way to play the game. Himself against the holding, chopping fools. Without a referee or rules.

Jerome Heavens did a one-eighty and jammed with both hands. "How'd you like that?" The golden retriever said nothing. It gave no sign of transmitting to its masters. It tipped the tennis ball with its nose toward Jerome Heavens. He threw its ball against the fence at the far end of the school yard. He stood at the foul line, pounding his dribble on the asphalt, while the golden retriever ran after the ball as if it was nothing but a dog.

He had not believed the lawyer at first. He had waited outside Dr. Chester's three times while the whore was there, but Mr. Boy Friend did not come. The third time, he followed the whore to the massage parlor. Mr. Boy Friend did not come again, but the fat doctor did. The fat doctor he had told about Esubio Chabchap, M.D. The fat doctor who had told Dr. Chabchap about him. The fat doctor had not admitted it at first. Then he admitted it. The fourth time he followed the whore from Dr. Chester's, she met Mr. Boy Friend at the Blue Horizon.

"Mind if I shoot?" A bald fool with Kareem goggles had come on the court.

Jerome Heavens pounded his dribble on the foul line while the fool moved into the corner. He pounded it while the fool loosed a one-hand push. The fool's elbow floated. The fool had no rotation. The fool had no idea the way that things must be. Jerome Heavens rebounded the miss when it clanked off the rim. He threw it where he had thrown the golden retriever's ball.

"What the hell's the idea?"

Jerome Heavens pounded his dribble.

"This a free country, man. You got the bill of sale for this basket?" "When I'm done, it's your turn." Jerome Heavens glanced from the three-on-three game to the Blue Horizon and back. The players argued. *You on the line, man. No, man, no. You on the line*; I *seen it. How you gonna see it, standin where you standin? Jimmy block your view.* A fool with a red headband pointed at the chest of a fool in a cut-off 49er jersey. A fool with purple-and-gold Karl Malone's was in the face of a fool with dreads and a Van Dyke. *You sayin I lie? I sayin you dint see me on no line. You on the line*; *you on the line*; *gimme that damn ball, blood.* Each fool argued like he could not understand the other fool did not believe one word he said. They would argue forever if they argued that way.

"You crazy, man? I just want to shoot."

Jerome Heavens cocked his thumb. He pointed his index finger at the Kareem goggles. "Bang." The golden retriever trotted back with the ball in its mouth. It flopped down with its head between its paws and let go of the ball. It nosed it toward Jerome Heavens.

"You come on now ..." Jerome Heavens threw the tennis ball to the far end of the school yard, a little closer to the gate. "... I'll rip out your tongue."

"You sick, man. You know that?"

The fool was not as smart or as devious as the golden retriever. But he walked after his ball.

Jerome Heavens picked up the rhythm of his dribble as if he was stitching himself to the school yard. The sky had darkened further. The wind had grown sharper and colder. Soon he would be alone in the school yard. He would watch the last light go out in the Blue Horizon. He had watched for three days. He could not enter the Blue Horizon, his mother had commanded, without watching it well. He could feel the correctness of the time forming, adding on, filling out within him and without him, until time and place and he had fused; and the act — the required act — the sacred and professional erasing — followed.

His mother had warned they were watching. The closer he had come to the Blue Horizon, the more this watching increased. The longer he held his ground, the more their agents multiplied. The more committed he became, the more forms their watchers assumed. They shadowed his steps with dogs and goggled fools. His van was always in their sight. They had cameras that snapped pictures through walls and microphones that picked up thoughts and powders they slipped into coffee so you slept 1000 years. It was necessary that the correctness was forming. It was righteous that the erasure occur.

Let them and their microphones and powders play.

Let them look him in the eye.

The golden retriever nosed the ball. Jerome Heavens threw it closer to the gate again. Once or twice more and he would have the golden retriever chasing the ball out the gate into the path of a car.

§

The laundry room of the Blue Horizon was on the top floor. The laundry had two coin-operated washing machines and two coin-operated dryers. It had a machine that sold boxes of detergent and bleach and one that changed a dollar. A puddle crossed the floor and the air steamed. Discarded magazines sat on the window sills: *U.S. News and World Report*; *Motorland*; *Focus*.

Stanley Doone watched gray water pour into the sink. It had been a strange few days. Some asshole was leaving messages on his answering machine. "I know who you are." "I am without fear." "You will pay and pay." At first, he had thought the messages a wrong number. But he could not imagine whose number the messages could be correct for. And the messages were not all. Some asshole would buzz his apartment, but when he buzzed back, no one came in. The manager said faulty wiring caused the buzzing. Fuck faulty wiring. That did not explain the brass flap to his mail box ripped from its hinges, twisted in half, hurled onto the floor. And since Tisa had told him about the insurance company's cameras, whenever he went out, he felt someone watching him.

The gray water slowed to a trickle. Stanley Doone tried to center, like Tisa would say, in his moment. Like his clothes in the washing machine, his self was about to shift cycles. The expectation was that both he and they would emerge brighter and improved. There was this difference, though, between life and washing machines. With washing machines you knew the order of the cycles. Wash before Rinse. Rinse before Spin Dry. In life, you never knew the fucking order. You only knew the cycles would change.

Soon his case would settle. Then he would marry Tisa. The impending impacts felt like two Brahma bulls bearing down on him from opposite directions. The settlement seemed easier to manage. The role of money was clear. When he went for burgers, he would not have to worry about ordering blue cheese and bacon. The next time he snapped a Converse lace, he could buy another pair. He would have the time *Lunacies and Failures* needed. Its appearance would assure his place in history. It would win him applause. It would prove his belief in his singularity had not been crazed. It would bring him fucking everything.

Fitting Tisa into the picture was trickier. It was like Cezanne had set this still life and, before he was back at the easel, someone had plopped an extra apple on the plate. The apple might be juicy, but it could fuck the whole design. He was not certain where this marriage idea had sprung from. But they had come down Mt. Tam with talk of it as integral to their afternoons as espresso and Madeleines. Marriage was not out of the question. He could see its pluses. He could concentrate more deeply on *Lunacies and Failures* if he had someone to do laundry, cook meals, make his fucking bed. Marriage could enrich his work by providing him a more rounded outlook, greater sense of purpose, connection to a broader stream of mankind. And there was nothing wrong with having Tisa want him. She looked hot. She listened good. She even had this old fashioned side. Like she had apologized for what had happened on the mountain. She promised it would not happen again. He would have loved it again, but Tisa said he should not take her for granted. They should wait until they married. Then they could do it all the time.

Stanley Doone's main concern was haste. Tisa's desiring him reminded him that other women would. He did not want his opportunities limited before *Lunacies and Failures* brought him all on which he counted. In his favorite comic book story, fifty healthy, intelligent, handsome men and fifty healthy, intelligent, beautiful women are selected by the leaders of a doomed Earth to be frozen into suspended animation for a lengthy rocket ship flight to a distant planet, where they are to awake, still youthful, vibrant, potent, and create a superior world. One man arranges to wake early. He disconnects the life support systems of the other men. He defrosts one woman at a time. When he gets bored, he kills her and defrosts another. Stanley had never forgotten the look on the rocketeer's face as he lingered over the suspended animation chambers, pondering his next choice — Blonde? Brunette? Redhead? — as if at a Baskin-Robbins counter — rum raisin? Butter crunch? Chopped chocolate? Over the years, his imagination had repeatedly screened the scene, recasting as the rotting men and enslaved women, anyone who had ever laughed at him.

"I hope I'm not disturbing." Mrs. Kopolwitz pulled her wagon toward the second washer. "I have these things to run." "The more the merrier," Stanley Doone said.

"Our son Myron is in town, scouting locations. He'll be taking us to dinner, I'm sure. I want to make a good impression." "Have a terrific time."

"Myron is so busy with his television. Did I mention his latest show? These young people share a beach house at Malibu, and each episode they spray a new strain of flu virus into the air filtration system. Whoever's left standing wins the grand prize. Where he gets these ideas is beyond me. His father and I, let me tell you, were always level-headed. Well, we grew up in different times. You should let me show Myron your book. He may have a suggestion."

"That is very kind. But I don't show my work till it is done." "You creative types! Always afraid someone will rob you blind. Well, don't say another word. Don't think I don't understand about being careful." Mrs. Kopolwitz hugged an armful of undergarments. "Did you hear Mrs. Frimmel, in 411, is back in Presbyterian?" Stanley Doone had not heard.

"Cancer of the breast. The poor thing. And a hot spot on her humerus. Such a shame. If there is anyone you would think is made of iron, it is Gertrude Frimmel."

Stanley Doone's machine had stopped. He peeled his laundry from the wall of the inner chamber and carried it to the dryer. The steam pressed against him like a cat.

"By now, I don't worry," Mrs. Kopolwitz said. "I am not afraid of death. I only pray, when it comes to my near and dear, there is little pain."

Stanley Doone placed two quarters in the dryer. He pushed the plunger. Slowly, with a muffled thud, the drum revolved. His laundry flopped about, rested and flopped again. The speed increased and, with the speed, the heat and, with the speed and heat, the drying. Through the circular glass, shirts and pants were indistinguishable. All that was in motion was a blur, flung from wall to wall.

"My life has had its sorrows, but it has had its joys." Mrs. Kopolwitz stared out the laundry room window. "Death just means an end to all that life has put me through. I am angry it's so final, though. I could see being dead five years, ten years, okay, one hundred years. But being dead forever. Never not being dead. Never, ever, not once having Morris hold my hand again. One hand-holding. Is that too much to ask? Couldn't there be some other arrangement? Some way out or some concession? You're a smart fellow, Mr. Doone. Is that any way to run a railroad? You want people to behave, you ought to offer something, am I wrong?"

Stanley Doone stood beside Mrs. Kopolwitz. The window was streaked with dirt. Each revolution brought the dryer's muffled thud. He did not know which of the pencil-eyebrowed faces peering up at him in the lobby was Mrs. Frimmel. He did not want to know. The settlement was his ticket to board the rocket for the distant planet. With all systems prepared for blast-off, he did not want one more distractive ounce asserting gravitational pull.

A player remained under the lights of the basketball court across the street, pounding his dribble on the foul line, pounding and pounding and pounding.

§

Tisa Rio did not scream.

She had seen the fuzzball when she came into the workout room, but she had been thinking about Princeton settling Stanley Doone's case. She had been thinking that, when Stanley had his money, he would be able to do anything and that, if this was to include her, she had to act. She did not think that fuzzballs were never in the workout room. She did not consider how unusual it was for this fuzzball, which was in a room that never had fuzzballs, to have accumulated around a length of peculiarly colored telephone cord, in a room where stray lengths of telephone cord never lay about.

She had lingered over her CD choice, still thinking. The money would give Stanley ideas. People would learn about the money and get ideas about him. Stanley was not exactly the most practical guy in the world. There was no telling what trouble he could get into. He could use a level head around. It wasn't only her who would be making out when she moved their relationship to the next level.

While she had been having these thoughts, her subconscious must have been thinking about the fuzzball. For suddenly she was confronting the image that resulted from the transformation of the fuzzball that was not into the dead rat that was.

The dead rat that had been eaten by other rats.

The fuzz was the fur.

The phone cord was the naked tail.

Toward the front were the vertebrae and rib cage, stripped of flesh, the color of boiled crayfish.

Tisa Rio made herself look. She made herself identify and register. It was as if the harder she looked, the more clearly she identified, the more firmly she planted the vision, the less meaning it would have, the less horror or terror or revulsion. The more it would be only what it was: a piece of trash on the workout room's floor.

She walked down the hall to the pantry. She brought back a whisk broom and dust pan, a bucket of hot water and rag, a spray bottle of ammonia and paper bag. She prodded the carcass into the bag with the whisk broom. When she did, she saw the maggots swarming. She sprayed the maggots with ammonia. When their swarming had stopped, she swept the maggots and fur and tail into the dust pan and dumped them in the paper bag. She scrubbed the floor with the rag and hot water and ammonia. She scrubbed until the floor was clean. She dropped the whisk broom and dust pan and bag into the garbage.

Then she washed her hands. She let the hot water run until she could not stand it. She scrubbed until her fingers were red. She was proud she had been so calm and thorough. She made herself remember everything.

The fluffy, gray-brown fur.

The hairless, bloody tail.

The miniature spinal column with its delicate ribbing.

Then she remembered. The rat had no head. Somewhere, in her penthouse, nibbled clean of eyes and lips, was the gleaming skull. Somewhere, other rats were dying, ready to be stripped of their own flesh, having gorged on the poisoned tissue.

Chapter XV.

The undercarriage banged. The silver Porsche shook and zipped on.

It had been in the center of his lane. Humped and raw and bleeding. It was already dead. Too big for a cat. Probably a dog. The bus had been on the right, and he was doing seventy-five; and it was too late to swerve.

A piece of carcass must have torn off on the engine. The longer he drove, the more it burned. The more it burned, the more it smelled. Thick and sweet and choking. Princeton Gutkin was glad to reach Ocean Beach and its salt air.

He walked where the sand was firmest. On his right was the ocean and on his left the sea wall. Beyond the sea wall, across the Great Highway, had been Joyland. His parents had taken him to Joyland for the roller coaster and carousel and fun house. His favorite amusement had been Laughing Lulu. Laughing Lulu was a mechanical cackling, fortune-telling crone. You put your nickel in the slot, and Laughing Lulu pushed a card at you. No matter what your fortune said, Laughing Lulu cackled.

But Joyland had been torn down. A developer wanted condominiums there. The developer did not know the land was too unstable for foundations, that the first winter's storm would level six months' construction, that people would not seek shelter where the wind drove sand like buckshot through the air. Now, beyond the sea wall, on the empty land, teenagers drank beer and played radios proportioned like aircraft carriers. At the sea wall's foot, four black-mustached men sat on a blanket with two red-bandanna-ed women. One of the men strummed a guitar and was singing "Vaya Con Dios." One of the men was vomiting red wine, and one of the women was comforting the vomiting man.

"So what does it mean?" Panda had said, handing him the slip of pink paper, "While You Were Out" on which she had written, "'Tonight the nuns are avenged.'"

"What're you talking about?"

"He said you'd know."

"Who said? You didn't get a name?"

"The man. Who called and left the message. He wouldn't leave a name. Is this, like, one of those Mystery Weekends, where the guests go to a spa in St. Helena, and someone plants clues about who killed the Earl?"

"What did he sound like, this man?"

"You want to know the truth?" Panda fiddled with an eyelash that was coming unglued. "Freaky as Jocko the Dog-Faced Boy."

The beach was black with oil from a tanker that had foundered. Long-necked birds stabbed beaks into the sand. Flies flitted across the debris of the tide line. Soon, Princeton Gutkin thought, Jerome Heavens will contact Stanley Doone.

He had begun to doubt it would happen. Every few days, Jerome Heavens had reported his nearly non-existent progress. He was searching for Stanley Doone but had not found him. He had found Stanley Doone but was studying his habits. He had learned Stanley Doone's habits but was planning his mission. When Princeton Gutkin hinted prompt action might be desirable, he heard about the heebie-jeebies on Jerome Heavens' tail. Gutkin had tried patience. But he had also considered the viability of a breach of contract action based upon a hired assassin's failure to perform.

Panda's news had caused Princeton Gutkin no regret or guilt. Stanley Doone had acted. He had acted. Now it was Jerome Heavens' turn. Hey, it could not be helped. Whatever the crazy bastard did. Their actions had occurred individually, naturally, one in response to another, the result of GOD'S WILL or the SINS OF THEIR PAST LIVES or the POSITIONS OF THE PLANETS or their RELATIONSHIPS WITH THEIR PARENTS BEFORE THE AGE OF THREE. Many explanations were available without finding fault or attaching blame.

The beach was no place for worrying. The beach was for fun. His parents would spread their towels and plant their umbrella and put their lunch basket in the shade. His mother would take out her *Saturday Evening*

Post and chuckle at "Hazel." His father would strip off his shirt to work on his tan. And he, Princeton, would build sand castles at the water's edge. His were the best on the beach. High towered and multi-turreted and drip-steepled. Thick walled and deep moated and canaled to block and channel the ocean from the castle's core. But the next afternoon, no matter how deep he had dug or how high he had piled, his castle had vanished without a ripple in the sand.

Funny, Princeton Gutkin thought, the way things turn out. Take Justice Vineland, for instance. Charles Evans Vineland, before his appointment to the bench, had taught anti-trust. He was one of those professors law students held in awe. Hair as white as purity, eyes piercing as sin. Vineland dressed in Savile Row, rode a chauffeured Jag, had an oil-heiress, *Vogue*-covergirl wife, who looked like she could give it to you six different ways, then roll out of the rack, and hostess a sit-down dinner for the College of Cardinals.

Vineland had this creed. There was an elite, of which he was one. Then there was everyone, of which there was you. He would announce the case for discussion. Then he would lean across the podium, rap a finger on the seating chart, mispronounce some student's name, and challenge "Agree or disagree?" Whatever choice the schlub made, Vineland battered him. Shifting facts, hurling hypotheticals, threatening, pleading, lying even, Vineland forced the schlub to abandon his belief. No matter how reasonable it seemed or how firmly the student tried to hang on, Vineland reduced that belief to crud. "Care to wager $100 on your position?" Vineland had taunted before demolishing one of Princeton Gutkin's arguments. "No? Well, then, how about backing mine?" And with that, Vineland demolished the case he had just made.

Vineland was in his second term when the Council for Judicial Qualifications petitioned for his removal. The charges varied. He did not speak to his brethren. He slept through oral arguments. He refused to debate or draft opinions. He appeared at the governor's inaugural ball wearing earrings shaped like baboons. He publicly urinated on his shoes. Interestingly, Princeton Gutkin had noted, at no time prior to the proceedings had any of Vineland's votes been the subject of debate. In fact, ninety-two percent of the time he had been with the majority.

Sand dollars crunched below his feet. A brown gull ripped the innards from a crab. The longer Princeton Gutkin walked, the fewer people strolled the beach. Soon, the only people were one hundred yards ahead. A fog had blown in and screened them. The fog had bleached the people an identical color. It had blurred their sizes and shapes. The exploding waves obliterated all sound. The people hovered in the middle distance, indistinct, undefined, never drawing closer, never pulling away. He stopped and stared at the ocean. He realized he had reached the continent's edge. He thought of the uncountable generations of Gutkins who had lived and died to place him on this spot. Ash and Beppo and Ash's Ashes backwards, trekked across mountains and oceans and centuries, grown upwards off knuckles, clambered down from trees. Many words had been spoken, deals dealt, breaths spent. He wondered how many Gutkins had executed a plan as slick as his. He doubted a hell of a lot. He pitied the rest their timid, stunted imaginations.

It occurred to him that, given his having posted himself as a Descendant Free Zone, the achievements of those trekking, clambering Gutkins ended here with him. If their lives had any meaning, his was it. And if, giving himself the benefit of considerable doubt, that did not seem the likely outcome of any sensible creator's master plan, so what? Sure, it took a certain amount of chutzpah to say, "Okay, thanks a lot, guys; but there will be no more; it's over"; but he could live with that. No one had put a gun to anybody's head at any stage of the generational march and commanded the continued pumping forth of sperm, unhindered from its doing its biologically favored duty. They had been grown-ups, making their own decisions. And if anyone before him had come to a similar conclusion and denied him his turn in the box, he wouldn't have been around to complain; so, hey, who was kidding who? Who was he hurting? It could even be his saying that the game had gone on long enough was, itself, saying something.

The sea was a grinding stone, biting through the shore. The sun was a vibrant disc, slicing through the fog.

§

"Tonight?"

"Tonight," Tisa Rio said again.

Stanley Doone was at his drawing board. Tisa sat on the edge of his bed, watching him look back at her through the sheets of clothes-pinned pages. He had not expected Tisa. When his buzzer rang, he had thought it another false alarm. Or co-tenant whose failing vision or palsied limb had caused the wrong button to be struck. Now he knew why she had come. "Terrific."

"Most marriages I know, the bride and groom should have registered for ball bats and rocks instead of linen napkins and Dansk fondue sets. But we have such incredible empathy, I said to myself, 'Why wait another minute?"

He did not move toward her. "Marriage is ... Yeah, really."

"This morning, I knew it was time. Princeton has been acting so weird. You know what he told me before he left the house? Just this El Sicko dream. Me and him have moved in with his parents. Me and his mom spend all day watching *Bewitched* re-runs on 'Nick at Night.' Him and his dad stroll around in matching bathrobes, blowing on tomato soup to get it cool. You ever hear anything so weird? You think I could have a serious relationship with someone who dreamed something like that? Brrr." Tisa Rio hugged herself and, teeth chattering, fell backwards on the bed. "Princeton *hates* tomato soup. He doesn't *own* a robe. His folks are *dead*, for God's sake. You won't believe it; but when we met, that man was dynamite. Now all he does is visit libraries."

"I own a bathrobe, man, you know. Orange terry cloth." Silent, lying on her back, arms folded on her chest, Tisa reminded Stanley Doone of the spacewomen in the suspended animation chambers. He wondered if she would have been his first choice to defrost. "My work requires research too."

"I totally respect your honesty." Tisa Rio sprang up. "But your work is creative. It has meaning for the ages. All Princeton cares about is money. He's so narrowly focused."

Stanley Doone looked from Tisa to his drawing board, where his characters waited for him to continue their adventures, through which would be delivered the message that a grateful world would welcome. "You sure tonight is the best time?"

"It's driving me crazy. Us living apart."

"Me too, man. But the way I'm fixed ..."

"You won't know I am around. If it's me invading your space that's got you worried, I can stay with Princeton till we can handle a place of our own. We don't even have to tell anyone we're married. Like our hearts will be together, though a city apart."

"That's, you know, hardly being man and wife."

"Try thinking outside the box, Stanley. Haven't you heard? It's a the eighties. God, for the past six months, Princeton and me've been roommates more than anything. He's too busy to want to bang my bones. If, now, he changes his mind, tough weenies. I will tell him I am busy too."

"Won't your parents mind missing the ceremony, man? I thought mothers liked that trip. Organs, lace, tossing the fucking bouquet."

"We'll send my folks the video. That way, they'll have the thrill of being present, plus the viewing comfort of their own living room."

Mr. Rabie smashed a bottle on the wall.

"Good. I'm glad that's settled. Now, I've got to pick up things. I'll be back in an hour. Brush off your best suit, sweetie. Shave. We can zip up to Tahoe and be back before anyone knows we're gone. If we make a couple lights, maybe we can sneak in some sack time." Tisa Rio looked back before closing the door. "Listen, Stanley, relax. You'll feel lots better once this is done."

§

Jerome Heavens came out of his van.

He wore his black suit jacket, black pants, white scorched shirt. His rainbow watch cap was pulled toward his eyes. He had taken two hits of sinsemilla. He had listened to "Round Midnight," "Ruby, My Dear." His body was layered to enter the Blue Horizon. His mind was lined to perform the required acts. He had loaded his Walther.

The whore had left fifteen minutes before. No one else had come out of the Blue Horizon. No one was on the street. Jerome Heavens knew someone was watching him. Despite the night and blackness. Despite the rhythm and smoke. He was not surprised to see no one when he spun around. The mantis had not seen anyone. The fat doctor had not seen anyone. But someone had been watching them.

He crossed the street. The floor of the vestibule was marble. The apartment buzzers were sunk in the north wall. The safety-glassed door was straight ahead. He had come this far before. Now he had to penetrate. But if he pressed a buzzer or put a shoulder through the safety glass, people would fill the hall.

Father Dynamite had taught that every act had its required spirit. If one part of the performance did not possess that spirit, another act was being performed. A speck left on his toilet bowl meant its scrubber had been inadequately respectful to be his bowl's devoted scrubber. A loose thread in the fringe of his prayer shawl meant its knitter was insufficiently grateful to be his shawl's worthy knitter. Someone, Jerome Heavens thought, on a sacred and professional mission would not allow trickery or violence to get him through a door. And he had to be on a sacred and professional mission. Why else had his mother guided his way? For what other reason was he followed? What else caused him to stand in the vestibule? It could only be his mission.

Beyond the glass, in narrow cubes braced one against another, the yellow air grew darker and more narrow the further it retreated from the street. In the cubes, specks of dust rose and fell and idled. Strange birds had been flocking in the city. The birds were black as grackles; but their beaks were sharper and more jagged than a grackle's beak; and on each bird's foot were twelve razor claws, which no grackle ever had. The birds' call was raw and as piercing as the horns which put the sword to Jericho. The birds were blunt-headed and club-bodied, the height and weight and density of English bulldogs. The wind that stirred with the beat of each bird's black wings moved with a force as if accelerated by a drop from a peak which crested at a point beyond all kindnesses and caring. The birds settled on the playground. They perched across the top bar of the swing and on the teeter-totter's highest arm. They thumped their wings and hooted and loosed their parasitic droppings into the sandbox's grit.

At the far end of the corridor, in a cube of air as darkly yellowed as a kris of Aztec bone, the doors to an elevator opened. Two small figures pulled two tiny wagons from it. Jerome Heavens did not blink or breath. He was in awe at the correctness of this intervention. He was inspired by its grace. At the same time, he took nothing for granted. He knew the figures could be double agents. He was aware they could vanish before they got to him.

The lock sprang at the figures' touch.

"Let me help," Jerome Heavens pulled open the front door.

"We've had plenty practice," Coach Kopolwitz said. "Repetition is the key. Run it till they stop you." "You should be careful. It is turning wet out there. It's becoming dangerous." "Wet, dry, hot, cold. The field's the same for both elevens."

"Come along, dear," Mrs. Kopolwitz said. "The gentleman is trying to get by." "I am on a sacred and professional mission," Jerome Heavens said. "I assist the forgotten and cast down. I right the wronged and correct the unclean." "I do hope you can do something for Mrs. Filippi. The poor thing's been coughing since four a.m. Or Mr. Dawn. What that man suffers from his lungs. Oh my, when I think of all the people who could use your services." "Let's get a move on," Coach Kopolwitz said. "If we hustle, Myron can get us back for the final quarter." Jerome Heavens watched as, frail hand in frail hand, still pulling their tiny wagons, the figures descended the front steps of the Blue Horizon. In the shadows, now, a red sports car waited. It rumbled in its throat. It rocked from side-to-side. When the sports car had absorbed the figures and their wagons, it leapt forward, its tail lights flaring like Satan's eyes.

With each step drawing him further from the street, Jerome Heavens heard his mother cooing to him, out of sight, beyond his reach, like a swallow nested in the rafters of a vermin-ridden barn. The loss of his mother had been a talon ripping his soul. He had been rent so rawly he had doubted he would ever mend. It had been so long since he had been with his mother. So long since they had danced.

§

Stanley Doone still sat at his drawing board.

His method was to begin with a story's last panel. He had come to this approach when he had realized he chose the stories to be included in *Lunacies and Failures* because of their endings. He wanted endings that grabbed. Endings that shocked and riveted. The seeping gas. The ashes in twin urns. The starved and shrunken baby.

Once he had selected a story — or, rather, once an ending had won selection for the story it appended — he had only to render a panel that would have such an effect upon a reader. The shock. The riveting. The ramming of the cold blade down the fucking throat. And once he had achieved this panel, he would know what panel had to precede it. The panel that would lead a reader to such apotheosis. And once he had that panel, he would know the one before it. So he would go on — or, rather, would be drawn on — backwards, ceaselessly backwards — learning where the entire story came from, uncovering origins, baring secrets, solving mysteries, building toward the start, towards freshness and the desirable, clean slate. Then, at some point — suddenly, always suddenly — he would know his first panel, the precise point of calm, where peace was always at hand, where possibilities were infinite, where dawn was eternally breaking; and he would jump to it and commence working toward his already existent end — panel-by-panel-by-panel — often working now in both directions, from the end and from the beginning, two railroad lines laying tracks across a continent from opposite coasts, awaiting the unifying golden spike.

The beginning was important too. It set the reader in motion — caught the eye, invited in, put at ease — then gave the quick push down the slippery slope. It let things start to happen — things you didn't know, things where choices must be made, things which took off helter-skelter, no return possible — and pulled you along and pulled you along until you connected with the fucking end. But these middle things, these connections, seemed arbitrary and free-floating and of less consequence than the beginning, which was almost a given, and the ending, which was given too. Stanley Doone felt he could add or subtract scenes in the middle at will or graft on scenes from other stories entirely, so long as he had the proper beginning and, most importantly, the end. So long as his ending was clear and strong and left the reader shaking, shuddering, all preconceptions defiled, exhaling fucking "Wow!"

He was working on a story about an All-American pitcher, whose promise had been unfulfilled. One night, in full uniform, the pitcher had returned to his college stadium, the scene of his greatest victories, and placed his scrapbooks and trophies beside the mound. Then, one toe on the rubber, he blew out his brains.

Should the last panel freeze the pistol barrel against the temple, unfired? Or should the corpse sprawl, full moon lit, across the humped infield? Should gore drip from the gold statuary and stain the leather-bound pages? Those were the only choices. Stanley Doone wanted his final panel to be completed before Tisa returned. He wanted to be positioned to commence his backwards journey toward understanding and completion. That was the purpose of the panels' march. Why else would you have an ending but to teach you how you had arrived there? He reviewed each of the possible pictures. The cocked hammer. The akimbo arm. The sculpted Adonis, bat upraised, prepared for any assault.

For some reason, he found himself remembering an evening with his parents on a visit to Los Angeles. He could have been six. He could have been eight or twelve. His parents had lived for some years in Los Angeles before he was born, and many old friends had come. The Melseys. Red and Arlene Bunch. Jerry Chinkowski and Mary Ellen. Yan and Yuri Ginkgo. He remembered nothing about the evening except the presence of his parents' friends. He remembered that the restaurant at which they met had been dark. He had no idea why he was remembering. These people had existed; they had been together; that was all. It was not the evening in the restaurant with the Mesnicks, who were visiting his parents from Washington; and Mr. Mesnick leant him his glasses so he could watch

Space Ghost on the television above the bar. He tried to recall scenes from the evening in Los Angeles. He tried to see his father clasp Obie Melsey's shoulder. He tried to see his mother kiss Mary Ellen Chinkowski's cheek. He remembered that Obie Melsey, who had been in the war, had sent him a parachute. His mother had stored the parachute in the basement; and whenever he had looked for it — once, twice, six, a dozen times — in boxes, in closets, on cabinets' top shelves — he had found curtains and table clothes and sweaters; but he had never found the parachute. He remembered that other children had been there. A white-haired boy with an egg-shaped head. A pig-tailed girl with a Raggedy Ann doll. Melseys or Bunches. Chinkowskis or Gingkos. Stuart or Brian. Bonnie or Caroline. The children had kept away from him as if he had been a well-known Judas goat. They had orbited the adults in tandem, sullen, scornful, annoyed at having been coaxed or coerced into this gathering, resentful of this curtailment of their liberty, scheming to run free. Now, remembering, he was uncertain if the children had actually been present or if some sadistic flaw in his memory had authored their inclusion in the scene only to make him feel shunned. He was incensed to have remembered the evening in the dark restaurant. Like so much else, the evening could have been superb. Like so much, about it, nothing could be done. He had been satisfied to have had the evening buried and forgotten, gone. He was, at the same time, fucking sad.

Stanley Doone got up from his desk. Five, six, seven ... turn. Five, six, seven ... turn. Prisoners in isolation would pace miles each day of their confinement. Do so many hundred push-ups on the floor. He wondered, if he had devoted himself to push-ups instead of *Lunacies and Failures* what, besides his collar size, would have materially changed. He worried again that settling for Tisa would cost him richer opportunities. He worried that her presence would interfere with *Lunacies and Failures*. He understood that the fear of success could make one set standards so high that they would never be met. He recognized the foolishness of fearing rewards because they would distract from work when it was rewards that work was designed to fucking bring. But imagining his ride to Tahoe with Tisa, he could only picture miles of road with falling rocks and hairpin curves and a pursuing Princeton Gutkin damning him for his treachery and daring. The covers of his comic books — the severed arm, the tentacles, the axe — mirrored the meager, fucking light.

As Stanley Doone paced, he fingered his pen. He thumped his mattress with his flatted palm. He turned the faucet of the sink and let the water trickle through his hands. He felt a need to capture and identify every detail of his room. The pen's grip. The mattress' musk. The water's fucking chill. Until this moment, he had not honored his room sufficiently. Together, they had withstood despair. United, they had battled toward greatness. He could not abandon his room until he had exhausted its fullness. Every second of its wonder ignored was an infinity lost. Every inch of its experience slighted was a galaxy untouched. Even the green fucking slime around the drain emitted the warmth of camaraderie and cause.

He stopped in front of his one window. He raised the frosted glass. Staring straight ahead, he tried to imagine the life Tisa and money would bring. Before him, beyond him, the darkness of the air shaft waited. Revealed, naked, it unwound like an undeciphered code. From it he had come and to it he would go. Eyes wide, mouth gulping, ecstatic, Stanley Doone thrust his head into the air shaft at the center of the Blue Horizon. He bent forward, both hands on the window's ledge, balanced on the fulcrum of his forearms, toes barely touching floor, bending toward the bottom, equally divided between in and out, light and dark, peering precarious, seeking silently the creatures dwelling in its Mariana Trench. The window seemed a portal beyond his present understanding, a threshold whose crossing required a courage he'd never possessed, its treasures tantalizing, unimaginable but close.

A pounding rocked his walls. A howl pounced upon his spine.
And pushed, he fell.

Th-th-hank you for s-s-seeing me.
E.C., MD
jt dockery

Chapter XVI.

"G'night, Mr. Gutkin."

"Night."

"Want me to lock up?"

"No, I'm expecting someone."

Princeton Gutkin watched Panda shake her can out of his office. He was glad to be alone. The walk on the beach had fixed him. He had returned without a doubt or worry. Any moment, the main stumbling block in his path would be reduced to *schmutz* in the furnace behind Jerome Heavens' gaze.

He could not see he had left one stone unturned. Even if Stanley Doone had told someone about his lawsuit, he had no heirs to carry it on. *I am sorry*, Princeton Gutkin heard himself explain to some nosy third cousin, *but without someone with the requisite degree of consanguinity, a cause can not survive a plaintiff's passing Regrettable but true.* And even if Jerome Heavens was unlucky enough to be nabbed and blabby enough to implicate him, no one would take his rantings, punctuated by his cockamamie accounts of his misbehaving heart and nipples. *See, officer, this fruitcake must have met Mr. Doone in my waiting room and blamed the poor soul, whose case I'd taken, for my rejecting his. Bad luck all around.*

Princeton Gutkin planted his feet on his desk. Best of all, his law practice boomed. Associating in Jerome Heavens had let him shake *Doone v. Keep-On Trucking*'s grip on his time. But because he had become used to the tension-cutting effort he had been spending on it — and needing to keep his mind off Stanley Doone's future — he had busied himself with ordinary matters. The result had been more releases signed, more checks deposited, more money pouring into his accounts and pocket. But the more cases he closed, the more he had to open to maintain this balance. So he had okayed this Mr. Graves' request for a meet after normal hours.

"Th-th-hank you for s-s-seeing me." The prospective client had brushed his hair and washed his hands. But his left eye twitched, his right nostril flickered, and his incisors had chipped a raw hole in his lower lip. He wore a blue corduroy vest and blue corduroy pants. But he had no jacket, and his feet bore orange flip-flops. One hand gripped a hand-tooled Mark Cross case and the other a brown paper bag was stained like it held a dripping, charred-but-raw Double Whopper.

"No problem." Princeton Gutkin had not quit hoping. Th flip-flops were a bad sign. But Grover Baltimore had bounced in barefoot and cashed out for eighty-five hundred. He picked up a yellow pad. "Address?"

"R-r-rincon Annex. General D-d-delivery."

"Phone number?"

"S-s-sorry."

"Any place I can leave a message?"

"Not at the m-m-moment."

"Well, what is the nature of your problem?"

"It is painful to d-d-discuss."

Princeton Gutkin controlled the urge to shout "What the hell, then, are you doing in my office?" "Anything you tell me, it's confidential."

"S-s-some m-m-matters ... E-e-elude r-r-rational d-discourse." "How'm I supposed to help, if I don't know the trouble? I mean, what're we talking here? Auto accident or alimony? Bailment or bad faith?" "C-c-coffee?" Mr. Graves eyed the office without changing expression. Melinda Moffett's tire, Lorelai Ono's dress, and R.B. Wimsey's ladder might have been banal family portraits hung the length of a tedious hall. "P-p-provided you will join me." If this yo-yo is out to score free eats, Princeton Gutkin thought, he is going to a lot of trouble.

Princeton Gutkin fumbled for the coffee room light switch. Upstairs, a typewriter struck. A vacuum sucked a floor's dust. Since Mr. Graves' arrival, he had not thought of Stanley Doone. The appointment was worth that, anyway. One case ended. Another began. In lawyer-books and lawyer-movies, that was how it happened. Paul Newman or Jimmy Stewart sat there, appointment book empty, calendar clear, when the new client walked in. MR. FALSELY ACCUSED. MS. TRULY DESERVING. Gutkin liked the idea of starting fresh. In his practice, he never thought of ends and beginnings. He never patted himself on the back for his job accomplished. He never sprang up for a shot at the next dragon. He was too busy stomping on the lizards crawling out of his drawers. This Doone *mishegas* was regrettable, sure. But after it was put to bed, he could learn from his mistakes, clean up his act, start over. In a way, hey, he was lucky it had happened to him.

He dumped a cigarette butt from a mug: OLD LAWYERS NEVER DIE. THEY JUST LOSE THEIR APPEALS. He scraped lipstick from one with a picture of Abe Lincoln. The Mr. Coffee had four inches in the pot. The sludge of grinds slid into the mug going to Mr. Graves.

Princeton Gutkin heard him whistle a passage from the Brandenburgs.

"I sh-sh-should have mentioned it." Mr. Graves' black case was in his lap. His brown bag was on his black case. "Th-th-three lumps. C-c-cream on the s-s-side."

"Don't give it a second thought."

Princeton Gutkin walked back down the hall. The typing had stopped. The vacuum rumbled. The customer was always right, but this joker knew how to take advantage. Still, let him tell his story. There could be some laughs in it. A few chuckles when he told it at the club. In this business, you had to have a sense of humor. This year's winner had been the walk-in — about ten months pregnant — wrapped in fifty pounds of blankets, looked like she roomed on Monkey Island. She only wanted to sue Napa State Hospital, the East Bay Regional Park District, and the original cast of *Beach Blanket Babylon.* When he gave her the boot, on her way out, apropos of nothing, she sniffed "It is so Richard Gere's baby."

The Cubelets were in the cabinet. So was the Cremora. Princeton Gutkin could not find a spoon, but he did not mind Mr. Graves stirring with an index finger.

The whistling, which had begun when he had left the room, stopped, as though interrupted by a thought or action.

"I-i-intentional I-i-nfliction of em-m-motional d-d-distress." Mr. Graves plopped cubes into his mug one at a time. He poured lightener from the jar.

"Excuse me?"

"I b-b-believe that is how those i-i-in your p-p-profession categ-g-gorize the n-n-nature of my c-c-contemp-p-plated litig-g-gation."

Princeton Gutkin put down his coffee. He had been accommodating with his time, generous with his libations, lavish with his condiments. And here he was being offered this turkey. Intentional infliction, for God's sake. Such bunk rarely paid. Proximate cause was tough. Damages speculative. And juries, without missing limbs to make them sniffle, not likely to be giving. If you even got to the jury. The standard of conduct to make a prima facie case was so demanding plenty judges non-suited you before you finished your opening statement. "So outrageous as to shock the conscience of a civilized man." How the hell did you prove that in an age when consciences, from all indicative factors, had acquired immunities as vast as the Russian steppes?

"My l-l-life is in d-d-danger."

"Hmmm."

"P-p-people p-p-plot to k-k-kill me."

"Yeah, right."

"At f-f-first, I b-b-believed only one m-m-madm-m-man involved. Then I f-f-found others i-i-implic-c-cated." Mr. Graves looked again at the tire, the ladder, the charred organdy taffeta. Now his expression had an authority that Einstein might have possessed. He radiated an understanding of the universe as no man before. He did not speak until Princeton Gutkin emptied his mug. "I am f-f-fighting back."

Princeton Gutkin wondered if entire segments of the population had become deranged due to climactic changes or the current economic state. "Tell you what. Put the highlights in writing. I'll run it by the partnership committee and be in touch."

"I c-c-can p-p-provide n-n-names and d-d-dates and d-d-documentation." "Unecessary. See, to be perfectly honest, I restrict my practice. No estates. No securities. No homicide rings." "You don't b-b-believe a word I've s-s-said."

"No, I belee you."

"You what?"

"I beleef ... beloove ..."

Mr. Graves sipped his coffee. "What d-d-do you know a-a-about ugu?" Princeton Gutkin shook his head. It had seemed as reasonable a question as any.

"A J-j-japanese b-b-blowfish. Tastes like p-p-pompano. A s-s-soup from thei-i- intestines contains s-s-sufficient p-p-poison to slay an entire b-b-banquet hall by p-p-pparalysis of the n-n-nervous system. A m-m-minute d-d-dose offers attractive f-f-features as an anaesthetic, though. One d-d-drop — in a b-b-beverage, for example — p-p-produces almost i-i-instant effect. The s-s-subject's s-s-speech s-s-slurs, his m-m-mind fogs, his b-b-body numbs. One commonly r-r-reported s-s-sensation is a f-f-frantic i-i-itching as if i-i-insects are c-c-crawling over one's b-b-body."

Coffee, Princeton Gutkin foggily thought, is a boover ... beaver ...

"A c-c-colleague warned me a m-m-man p-p-planned my m-m-murder. i-i-imagine the s-s-shock. I-i-imagine the f-f-fright. Weaklings m-m-might have c-c-crumbled. B-b-but I was strong. I s-s-stalked my s-s-stalker all the while he was s-s-stalking me." Mr. Graves' incisors chipped at his lower lip. The hole grew rawer and enlarged. "One afternoon, m-m-my quarry m-m-met another m-m-man. This p-p-person seemed l-l-legitimate, r-r-responsible, the r-r-respected citizen. Why, I asked m-m-myself, would s-s-someone that e-e-established d-d-dine with s-s-someone that i-i-insane. The a-a-answer was i-i-inescapable. The t-t-two were in league."

Princeton Gutkin wondered how those bugs had gotten under his shirt.

"The f-f-first m-m-man c-c-complained I had m-m-mistreated his organs. They will not t-t-trouble him again." Mr. Graves plopped the brown paper bag into the Out box on the captain's desk. "N-n-now I s-s-shall attend his p-p-partner similarly."

Princeton Gutkin felt himself pushed back. He felt the unknotting of his tie, his shirt's unbuttoning. His office seemed to recede, drawn like smoke into a vent, toward the chasm on the lip of Mr. Graves. The noise from the building, the street, the city, from near and far, the loud and soft, was vanishing. The light — even the variegated light — was falling away, bleached into a shrinking, standardized field. Against this universal dissolution, only Pritikin remained, inked of bone and wire before the empty, silent plain. Beppo's final attempt at advancement, Gutkin recalled, had been piano lessons. "Entertain associates and friends," the brochure had promised. "Be the life of any gathering." He saw his father, in his final days, arthritic, glaucoma-afflicted, the cancer working on his spine, bending forward on the bench, squinting through the shadows at the score, striking the keys that flung the music at the air: "Night and Day"; "Body and Soul"; "Always." With effort, Gutkin raised a hand toward something.

Mr. Graves swung the clasp on the Mark Cross case, monogrammed "E.C., M.D." The saws and scalpels glittered.

Chapter XVII.

This time, Tisa Rio did not release the buzzer until she had counted to one hundred. That creep, she thought. That double-crossing, four-eyed creep. For all he cared, she could count to a million, and he would not open the door. She knew all about roses rising from garbage and giving up attainment but she'd had it up to here with everything being transitory; and she did not feel the least reborn. In case Stanley Doone was camped out, grooving on the buzzer's steady drone, she fired a staccato burst. Then she left the Blue Horizon.

Her Porsche was parked beside a grate. Steam poured from it like Hell resided a foot below Jones Street. Okay, she thought. Maybe she was jumping to conclusions. Any second Stanley could come running up, frantic, breathless, afraid that he had missed her. From the cleaners where he'd left his suit. From the florists where he'd brought orchids to surprise her. From the pharmacy where he'd scored a career high in safes. She took the half-pint of brandy from the hip pocket of her jeans. She had swiped it from Princeton's liquor cabinet to keep her toes warm on the ride to Tahoe. She had taken a hit on the way to Stanley's and a second while pounding on the door. She took another now.

Stanley did not come running out of anywhere.

A black van was parked across the street. Flies buzzed around it. A golden retriever sniffed at the rear doors. The dog had a thick, matted coat. It gripped a yellow tennis ball in its jaws. The dog reared on its hind legs and scratched at the doors and whined. It trotted to the driver's side, lifted a rear leg, and squirted on the front tire.

"Right on, pup. Piss on 'em all." Tisa Rio extended her bottle toward the golden retriever.

The dog trotted to her and wagged its tail.

"Cheers." Tisa Rio held out the bottle. "We both got stood up, right? We're in this together." The dog cocked its head.

"Have it your way. We will play your little game." Tisa Rio knelt on the sidewalk at eye level with the golden retriever. She reached for the tennis ball.

The dog yanked its head away.

"Hard to get, huh?" Tisa Rio took another drink. Then she faked with her bottle and grabbed the ball with her opposite hand.

The dog backed away, thrashing its head from side-to-side and growling.

"God, guys are so possessive." Tisa Rio let go of the ball. She knew how the dog felt. When you thought you had something good, someone took it away. When you thought you had it back, they took it again. She wiped her hand on the sidewalk. "It's so slimy and yucky. I don't know why you want it anyway."

The dog lay down with its head between its paws. Its tail thumped back and forth.

"Hooray! A new position." Tisa Rio placed her forearms on the pavement and her chin between them. She could see the dog's purple gums. She could count the dog's warn, jagged teeth. She could smell the dog's foul breath.

It released the ball. It batted it with its nose toward Tisa Rio.

Tisa Rio batted the ball with her nose toward the shaggy beast. It opened its jaws.

§

"So, pop," Kirk Myron Kopolwitz slid behind the wheel, his mission, should he accept, get the folks home in time for *Cosby*. "Wha'd'ya thunk? Less than a dozen of these babies in the country. Tony Danza influenced his *paisans* to jump me up the list. Zero-to-sixty in 3.1 seconds."

"I did a 4.2 forty in full pads in 1939," his father said.

Kirk Myron Kopolwitz dug his nails into the Corinthian leather of his fresh-from-the-factory Zeus IV. He had added the "Kirk" for class before ABC had picked-up the pilot for his first series back in the dark ages — Buddy Hackett as an alien who lands in Nevada to check out American nuclear testing and ends up a lounge-act married to Charo. A beautiful concept, with political back story, powerful shit, real shit, true to his committed nature, just not about to put any suit in mind of the Port Huron Statement. But the network had slotted his baby against *The Waltons* when John-Boy was hotter than a boil on Loni Anderson's ass and dropped the option after six episodes. He'd thought the folks would've appreciated the gesture, not turning his last name into Kopp or Kipp or Klitoritz, but they had hardly noticed. He could puke rubies on the lamb's shank during the seder, and they would hardly notice.

"It's lovely, dear." His mother patted the back of his head. "And red is such a good color for you." "'Flamingo Mulch,'" Kirk Myron Kopolwitz said.

"Bishop Kronski wore red," his father said. "Made those mackerel-snappers look bigger. I ran for 187 yards against them in 1940."

Kirk Myron Kopolwitz considered his watch. He had been with the folks for seventy-five minutes. He loved them dearly, but the tension headache that blossomed every time they got up-close-and-personal was fire-bombing his right eye. He visited them; it visited him, almost a member of the family. And what about a family, each member a common ailment? Sister Sneeze. Brother Bronchitis. Mother Migraine. Father Flu. He could work with that. Their enemies could be a tribe of multi-colored vitamins. Maybe animated. Maybe Saturday morning for the kids. Maybe he was losing his mind.

"Whatever you say, pop. But if I pulled notices in the trades like this baby in *Road and Track*, I could retire us all to the eighteenth fairway at Kapalua. How'd that be? Play a round each morning after the kippers?"

"Your Uncle Howie played golf. He always was a little off. Football, there's a sport. Basketball. Baseball." His father thought it over. "Maybe ice hockey."

"How about *Celebrity Bowling*?'" Kirk Myron Kopolwitz half-whispered. The folks. God bless 'em. You can't live with 'em; you sure can't live without 'em. He never should have brought the subject up. They were set in their ways; nothing he could do to change them. He had offered Boca, Palm Desert, Cabal; they wouldn't let him move them one-inch out of their pest-house. His mother, afraid the other Q-tips would think them big-headed. His father, afraid he wouldn't keep up with the box-scores. And neither would consider him getting them wheels where they could get out, go places, make new friends.

So he's got this sit down with this lawyer controls this property worth half a look. This *Catalog of Crapola and Crazy-Making*, whatever. Could be *Twilight Zone* meets *Believe it or Not*. He comes up an evening early. Offers to take them anywhere they want; and the winner is — big surprise — The Yellow Pagoda, for the "Seniors Early Bird Special." "Mom," he tells her, "Cross my heart, it won't break me, we don't eat till six." "Save your money," she says. "Sweetheart, you never know when you may need it."

So, okay, the Yellow Pagoda. His mother compliments the shrimp-in-lobster-sauce and goes ga-ga over the pictures of each of the waitress' sixteen grandchildren — as if he doesn't get the message after Woo Number Four. His father occupies himself dropping chicken-fried rice on his shirt and naming the starting line-ups for every team in the Public League play-offs, 1958- to-'60. And he gets through knocking down a double Stoli before a Tsiang Tao with his chicken chow-fun, another double to wash down his almond cookie.

"Howard was a good husband and a wonderful father to the girls," his mother said.

"If he ever said anything worth hearing," his father said, "I was out of the room. Just don't talk to me about golf. When I was your age, I was playing two-on-two three hours at the community center."

And how about *Celebrity Two-on-Two*? Kirk Myron Kopolwitz thought. How about *Celebrity MIXED Two-on-Two*? Horace and Amy Grant versus Cazzie and Jane Russell? Cornbread and Elsa Maxwell taking on Big Country and Martha Reeves? He pinched the bridge of his nose. He was missing the boat again. He was missing the entire pier. Hope, the suits wanted. Faith and Charity, he thought. Three chicks. Fluffy hair. Big guns. T&A supreme. Been done, no? A thing with feathers then. Emily D. Hadda be in the public domain. Maybe that Ken Murray thingie. Entire cast of parakeets. No downside he could see but the bird seed and poop sprinkled on the Karastan. Better drop it before they hauled him to the funny farm.

He had gotten from the Blue Horizon to the Yellow Pagoda in six minutes forty-two seconds, nearly sixty ticks faster than he had made the run in his Viper. He bet he could beat that if he caught a break with the traffic. He glanced at his watch again.

His father looked at his watch too. "Okay, kiddo, show me what this sardine can can do."

§

This latest miracle had banished any doubt Stanley Doone might have held that he had been saved from the drownings for a purpose.

He lay on his back a mattress flung, who knew how long ago, or by which tenant, or for what half-mad reason, into the airshaft of the Blue Horizon. He did not know, how long he had lain there; but, from the color of the sky hung parallel above him, it could not have been very.

Slowly, Stanley Doone began to re-assemble understanding. He made his way, weak-kneed to a door, which opened into a basement. A flickering bulb lit it. Exposed wiring laced one wall. Iron-barred cages braced the opposite. They held the purged possessions of the tenants of the Blue Horizon. Skis that would never schuss again. Bowling balls which had picked up their last seven-ten split. Spoons and mashies, whose kerchiefed heads mourned the fairways they would never master. He saw radios the size of Babe the Blue Ox and televisions whose screens would have pinched Tinkerbelle and enough bedroom suites for a century of game show champions. He saw a bird cage that could not sing, a dog house as barren as Thebes, and an aquarium dry as the fucking Gobi.

Stanley Doone searched the cages as he might a Rorschach blot. He sensed that any cage, if unlocked, could unleash sufficient stories to save a harem of Scherazades. He could feel pulsations from tales that would break hearts and stimulate minds. All this content had been cast off, yet retained, as if its owners believed that reversals could occur, that opportunities could be regained, that they would, any day now, re-master slopes and lanes and fairways, that the lost parakeets and schnauzers, the guppies and black mollies would reclaim their habitats. The poignancy of this collective holding-on seemed to afford the Blue Horizon a weight that kept it from floating into the empty sky.

Stanley Doone viewed his place in the world with new precision. The corridor in which he stood, the cages beside him, another door at the basement's end, seemed perfectly placed. Each cage seemed a panel, whose contents he had to understand — as was each moment of time he passed through. The bottom of the air shaft, bordered by the inner walls of the Blue Horizon, had been a panel too. In fact, he had lain on the mattress, as the pitcher had lain on the mound in his story, but his laying had not been an end. He had survived; and now he was racing backwards, past these other panels, to uncover his beginnings.

He burst through the door, up half a flight of stairs, onto the sidewalk.

§

Tisa Rio rose from the golden retriever as Stanley Doone rushed from the Blue Horizon into the intersection, towards her. Neither saw the red — well, Flamingo Mulch — sports car flash through the stop light.

Tiso Rio saw Stanley Doone waft through the air and land in a privet hedge. She did not consider whether he had or had not suffered comminuted fractures, as he struggled to extricate himself. It did not factor into her considerations that a breatholyzer's results could entitle him to punitive as well as compensatory damages from the vehicle's driver.

"Hon," she said when she reached him, "you sure have possibilities."

Author's Afterword.

The weird thing is how much of this is true.

There was a fellow – not an M.D. – down the peninsula, I think – "Dr. Sex," the papers called him – who had women believing screwing him would cure some disease. I knew an orthopod who drew a suspension like Beaujack's for two patients who died from his knife. I knew a lawyer who, like Gutkin, lied to his clients to make himself look good. I knew a woman who worked in a massage parlor with rules like Tisa's. There was a guy on the California Supreme Court who lost his seat for behavior like Vineland's. The newspaper clippings Stanley stapled to his index cards were based on stories stuck inside my mind. Not to mention that a guy who co-starred in a B-movie with a chimpanzee was twice elected President.

As I said, I had a client who reacted like Jerome Heavens to a hernia repair. When a psychiatrist warned the operating surgeon about the client, the man left the state. The defense attorney refused to put his name on any document the client might see. The judge who had to approve the settlement couldn't sign it quick enough. As for me, one afternoon while the case was pending, I received a call from a medical malpractice attorney. My client also wanted him to sue his doctor. When the lawyer told the client that the hospital records said nothing about a transmitter having been implanted inside him, the client said I must have removed these references.

The lawyer thought I would want to know this turn of events.

You could certainly say that, to some degree, *The Schiz* was my attempt to master anxiety. (The phone call from the med mal attorney occurred more than thirty years ago, and I still hope to read that client's name on the obit page.) And in my own way, I reacted to the news of the client's nature like Princeton Gutkin. It became a fact to be used. What might someone do with such a client, I asked myself, within a story? Well, he might ... Then I just had to fill the other pages.

Certainly you could also call *The Schiz* an unfairly skewed view of the world. Certainly it is skewed. Certainly it does not fairly present all the views within me. (Did Nathanael West feel only one way about Hollywood?) Certainly I knew more lawyers and doctors, patients and clients who behaved more admirably than those I depicted. But this does not convince me I needed to make room for them in my book.

By the 1980s, it was clear to me that America was not working out the way it was supposed to. And each decade I re-read my book, my view seemed reasonable and valuable and I was glad I held to – and reinforced – it. Each time I paged through, I thought, WHEW! I have never read anything like this! That always seemed a good thing. Wasn't part of art picking up a thread of thought and seeing where it led you? When people asked me (or I asked myself) why I did not write a book about lawyers like John Grisham or Scott Turow, I would reply I had already written a book about lawyers and saw no reason to write one someone else could.

So here we are in 2016. The 1% are where they are. The 99% are where they are. The Mid-East is where it is. The polar ice caps are not even where they were when I began writing, and we may have as President a walking cesspool who makes me long for that chimp.

Oh, yes, Adele says I should say a few words of clarification about the dialogue. Originally, it had been laid out as neat and trim as Elmore Leonard's. But in converting from Word Perfect, which is how I write, to Word, which is how Milo reads, my computer must have judged correctives were in order and consolidated portions of certain conversations into a single paragraph. Milo, who thought these were choices of mine and approved of their "Altmanesque effect," exercised no overruling editorial decisions and returned them in a pdf to me.

I was initially taken aback. But then I was taken by the randomness of the computer's contribution. John Cage, I thought, would approve. Plus, the unanticipatable rhythmic shifts that resulted had the liberating effect of Free Jazz. And in terms of literary precedent, William Gaddis had replaced quotation marks with dashes, and Cormac McCarthy had eliminated such punctuation entirely, so I could feel I and my computer were making our own signatory contribution. Finally, as long as readers paid attention, they could figure out who was saying what. It might have been easier and more comfortable for readers, if I re-separated the speakers, but readers' "ease" and "comfort" was not what *The Schiz* was about.

Illustrator Biographies.

The rule was that each cartoonist_would receive only the chapter he or she was assigned. Our thought was that having multiple interpretations of the characters would, as Milo put it, "match the twisting/twisted kaleidoscopic narrative shifts of the story itself." Thumbnail descriptions of the characters were provided, but the cartoonists were free to ignore them. If a cartoonist asked for background or context, it was supplied. They were asked only to tone down the genitalia.*

The compensation we offered was scanty. Our gratitude is great.

Here, in the order in which their art appears, is a brief identification of each contributor.

Front cover: **François Vigneault** is a freelance illustrator, cartoonist, designer, and teacher (not necessarily in that order) living in Montréal, Québec. His comic *Titan* is available online and in print at Study Group Comics. Francois-Vigneault.com

Introduction and Afterword: **Austin English** is an artist and cartoonist living in Brooklyn. His books include *Christina and Charles* and *Gulag Casual.* His illustrations have appeared in *The New York Times* and his art has been exhibited internationally. DominoBooks.org

Prologue: **Josh Bayer** has worked in every visual medium from zines to television, but mostly comics. He is the creator/editor of *Suspect Device Comics*, the author of *Raw Power*, *Theth* and other comics. He teaches comics and visual art classes at Parsons School of Design. JoshBayer.com

Chapter I: **Shary Flenniken** is a Seattle-based freelance cartoonist, editor and screenwriter. She holds degrees in Multimedia Technology and Professional Teaching, and is best known as the creator of the *Trots & Bonnie* comic strip and as a contributor and editor at *The National Lampoon.* SharyFlenniken.com

Chapter II: **Eric Haven** draws absurd, bleak, violent comics. His books include *UR*, published by Ad/House, and *CompulsiveComics*, coming soon from Alternative. He was also a producer for *Mythbusters.* EricHaven.com

Chapter III: **Mark Bode** is a second generation cartoonist, living in the Bay Area. He has several successful comics to his credit, and has had gallery showings of his art and spray-can murals of his creation displayed around the world. MarkBode.com

Chapter IV: **Fred Noland** is an illustrator and cartoonist residing in Oakland. Buy hs comics. He needs the closet space. FredNoland.com

Chapter V: **R.L. Crabb** has been creating comics since 1981. His twice-weekly strip *It Takes a Village Idiot* can be viewed at RLCrabb.com

Chapter VI: **Casanova Frankenstein**, the creator of *The Adventures of Tad Martin*, lives in Austin, TX. Balancing his Fine Arts undergrad studies with a PhD in Metaphysics, he has been out to change the world since the day he was born under a bad sign, inside a barrel of butcher knives. TheArtOfFankastye.blogspot.com

Chapter VII: After serving in the Air Force, **Ted Richards** moved to San Francisco and joined the Air Pirates in 1970, later contributing to Gilbert Shelton's Fabulous Furry Freak Brothers. He is now an interactive creative director and Web developer in Silicon Valley. TedRichards.net

Chapter VIII: **James Romberger** is a fine artist and cartoonist who lives and works on Manhattan's Lower East Side. His graphic novels include *Aaron and Ahmed*, *7 Miles a Second* and *The Late Child and Other Animals*. He is currently completing the second volume of a comic book/flexidisc collaboration with his son Crosby, *Post York*. JamesRomberger.com

Chapter IX: **Jack Katz** has worked professionally in comics since he was a high-school student in the 1940s. Considered by some to have been the first graphic novel, his masterwork *The First Kingdom* was recently reissued by Titan Comics. JacKatz.com

Chapter X: **Ariel Schrag** is the author of the novel *Adam* and the graphic memoirs *Awkward*, *Definition*, *Potential*, and *Likewise*. ArielSchrag.com

Chapter XI: **Gary Hallgren** received a BA in painting and design in 1968, just in time to turn on, tune in and drop out. He dropped in with the Air Pirates Studio. He is currently ghosting the daily strip *Hagar the Horrible*. He lives in Massachusetts with his wife Michelle, a cat, five saxophones, and three Studebakers. GaryHallgren.com

Chapter XII: At age 21, **Dan O'Neill** became the youngest syndicated cartoonist in America with his strip *Odd Bodkins* in the *San Francisco Chronicle*. He later assembled The Air Pirates and launched an assault on Walt Disney. DanONeillComics.com

Chapter XIII: **Tyler Landry** is a cartoonist and art director who lives and works in Charlottetown, P.E.I., on the east coast of Canada. TylerLandry.tumblr.com

Chapter XIV: **Gabrielle Gamboa** is a San Francisco Bay Area cartoonist and illustrator. GabrielleGamboa.com

Chapter XV: **David Chelsea** is the author of the books *David Chelsea in Love*, *Welcome to the Zone*, *Perspective!*, *Extreme Perspective!* and a recent collection of his superhero character Snow Angel's stories. His webcomic *Are You Being Watched?* can be seen at WatchedComic.tumblr.com.

Chapter XVI: **J.T. Dockery** is a native Kentuckian, bourbon drinker, and comic book artist whose paper products include such titles as *In Tongues Illustrated*, *Spud Crazy* (with Nick Tosches), *DESPAIR* (vols. 1-3) and the serialized *HASSLE*. JTDockery.com.

Chapter XVII: **Aaron Lange** is a bartender and the author of the underground comix *Romp* and *Trim*, which are available from TheComixCompany.ecrator.com. He lives in Philadelphia and drinks coffee until his stomach bleeds.

***Editor's note:** According to the Canadian house that we originally wanted to print this book, their country's customs agents are all either total dicks or complete pussies when it comes to the visual depiction of genitals in the printed matter that crosses their border, regardless of which direction it travels. I personally find this difficult to believe of a nation as cool as Canada. One would think, regardless, that said agents would appreciate seeing positive depictions of themselves disseminated far and wide. Bob and I decided not to bet an entire print run of this book to find out.

Bob also reminds me that, before a single illustration was drawn, *The Schiz* was rejected by a self-described "small, family-owned printing business" who contacted us after we placed a call online for bids on printing the book, but backed out of our partnership on moral grounds after seeing just the text. The novel you are holding is officially "Too Hot for Aberdeen, South Dakota." —**MG**